The masked man had Amy.

"Stop! Police!" Jackson shouted. "Let her go! Now!"

He ran faster, not even certain they'd heard him over the sound of the scuffle. Jackson reached for his badge, then realized he'd left it with his gun back in the truck. The masked man dropped Amy and ran. She sank to her knees. Her hand reached inside her jacket as if searching for something.

"Amy!" Jackson shouted. He dropped to the ground beside her and grabbed her by the shoulders, just trying to steady her enough to pull the bag off her head. But a fresh scream tore from her lips and she struggled against him. "Hey, it's okay, I'm not going to hurt you—"

But the words had barely left his lips when her right hand darted up in front of his eyes. She was holding a small black canister of bear spray. The ring was wrapped around her finger. The nozzle was pointed directly at his face.

"Hey!" He let her go. "Put that away. It's me, Jackson—"

Amy yanked the pin and fired.

Maggie K. Black is an award-winning journalist and romantic suspense author with an insatiable love of traveling the world. She has lived in the American South, Europe and the Middle East. She now makes her home in Canada with her history-teacher husband, their two beautiful girls and a small but mighty dog. Maggie enjoys connecting with her readers at maggiekblack.com.

Books by Maggie K. Black

Love Inspired Suspense

Undercover Protection
Surviving the Wilderness
Her Forgotten Life
Cold Case Chase
Undercover Baby Rescue

Unsolved Case Files

Cold Case Tracker

Pacific Northwest K-9 Unit

Undercover Operation

Rocky Mountain K-9 Unit

Explosive Revenge

Visit the Author Profile page at LoveInspired.com for more titles.

Cold Case Tracker

MAGGIE K. BLACK

LOVE INSPIRED SUSPENSE
INSPIRATIONAL ROMANCE

LOVE INSPIRED® SUSPENSE
INSPIRATIONAL ROMANCE

Recycling programs
for this product may
not exist in your area.

ISBN-13: 978-1-335-59949-0

Cold Case Tracker

Copyright © 2024 by Mags Storey

For questions and comments about the quality of this book, please contact us at CustomerService@Harlequin.com.

® is a trademark of Harlequin Enterprises ULC.

Love Inspired
22 Adelaide St. West, 41st Floor
Toronto, Ontario M5H 4E3, Canada
www.LoveInspired.com

Printed in U.S.A.

The Spirit of the Lord is upon me, because he hath anointed me to preach the gospel to the poor; he hath sent me to heal the brokenhearted, to preach deliverance to the captives, and recovering of sight to the blind, to set at liberty them that are bruised.
—*Luke* 4:18

With thanks to Emily
my editor for ten years
for all the incredible books we did together

ONE

There was a man standing on the sidewalk across from the Clearwater Bookstore, staring at Amy Scout through the storefront window. She froze as her hands instinctively cradled the unborn child in her belly. This was the third time today she'd spotted the stranger with his imposing black and tan German shepherd outside the store, which was unsettling considering how deserted the tiny town in Northern Ontario was during the offseason. But if he was going to eyeball her then she was going to take down every single detail she could about him in return.

Amy grabbed her sketchbook and a charcoal pencil, letting her fingers find his face on the page. His beard was dark, and his jawline was handsome in an intimidating way. He had curly hair and a build that was muscular and strong. There was an intensity to his gaze, although in the gloomy light of the late afternoon she couldn't quite make out the color of his eyes.

As if sensing her gaze, the man turned and said something to his dog. Then the pair continued down the sidewalk, leaving Amy with just the charcoal picture of his face. She studied it a moment. There was something oddly familiar about him.

Had she seen him somewhere before? Was he there to hurt her? Did he have anything to do with Gemma's disappearance?

She had a whole lot of questions but absolutely no answers. Amy closed her eyes and prayed.

Lord, please keep me safe. Help me keep my baby safe too and bring Gemma home soon.

She had to believe her missing friend was still alive, despite that law enforcement had told her Gemma had probably drowned and her body might never be found. Two weeks ago, Gemma's empty car had been found submerged in a dangerous river, at the bottom of a steep waterfall near the town of South River, about an hour from Clearwater. Amy had no idea where Gemma had been going when she'd left the cottage that day or what she'd even been doing in that area.

It was like her best friend had been hiding something from her. Gemma had started going into the store early in the morning and returning there late at night after dinner, but she would never give Amy a straight answer when she asked why. There'd been some big secret, something that was bothering Gemma. Whatever it was, Gemma had refused to talk about it. She kept Amy in the dark and then she disappeared.

Amy closed the blinds firmly, locked the front door and switched the hand-painted sign in the window from Open to Closed. Her unborn daughter kicked within her and a smile crossed Amy's lips. The doctor told her this fluttering would become stronger and more frequent in the next six weeks before the child was born. To Amy the poking and prodding always felt personal, as if her child was trying to communicate with her. She liked it, and it made her feel less alone.

"Hello, Skye," Amy said. She couldn't remember exactly when in her pregnancy she'd named her daughter that, but it seemed to fit. The sky was immense and beautiful. It was peaceful at times, yet life-changing and powerful too.

"I'm just closing up shop now," Amy went on. She walked over to the front counter, opened the cash register and began to count the money. "Gemma still isn't here. But I want to make sure that everything is in tip-top shape when she gets back."

They'd been best friends since they met in seventh grade. Amy couldn't remember a time—day or night—when Gemma hadn't been willing to drop everything to be there when she needed her.

Vice versa too. Amy wasn't about to let Gemma down now.

"This place is a ghost town right now," Amy added. "Most of the stores are shut and the cottages are empty. But from the May long weekend to Labor Day, it's going to be packed around here. The lake will be crowded with boats, and there will be tourists and vacationers everywhere. Not to mention busloads of campers."

She moved from the cash register to restocking the bottled drinks and snacks in the minifridge, then started straightening the books on the shelves. The store itself was a former barn that Gemma had painted a bright turquoise. Oddly it always seemed smaller on the inside than it looked from the outside. In the main room they displayed newly released and bestselling books, along with DVDs and VHS tapes for rent since there was no cable television up here and the internet signal was weak.

A smaller room off to the side had floor-to-ceiling bookshelves filled with mostly used books, including an entire back wall dedicated to crime, cold cases and unsolved mysteries. It was also home to the store's resident conure parrot, Reepi Cheeps. The little bird was only a few months old. His name was a twist on a character from one of Gemma's favorite childhood books. The green and gray conure more than lived up to his name with constant cheeping and chirping, as he bounced around the high shelves. Reepi lived in the store during the warmer months and was allowed to roam free when it was quiet.

"See, I'm not alone," Amy told Skye, as she continued to tidy. It comforted her to talk to her daughter. "I've got a birdie and a baby on the way. Plus, we had a pretty good day, all things considered. We had twelve sets of customers, which isn't bad for a Tuesday in April. One of them even bought a couple of my postcards—the ones I drew of Reepi. I think I might paint him on the side of the building when the weather gets warmer. We can make him our unofficial mascot."

She just had to think positive, keep moving and not let herself consider that Gemma might not come home. It had been Gemma's idea to start selling Amy's sketches in the bookstore. When some of the customers balked at the sticker price, Gemma then started selling postcard prints of Amy's artwork alongside the originals. There was no way Gemma was about to let anyone haggle over the price of her best friend's art.

Gemma had always been protective. Maybe even overprotective. When Amy called her in a flood of tears to tell her that Paul—the man Amy had just eloped with—had turned out to be a liar and a conman who'd robbed her blind, Gemma had immediately driven through the night to pick Amy up and bring her back to the cottage.

That was long before Amy even realized she was pregnant with Paul's child.

She paused with her hand on a misplaced DVD as a sudden chill ran down her spine at the memory of the man who'd ruined her life...

It was my fault for being impulsive. I always jump into things without thinking.

And then I ended up prey to an evil man...

Skye kicked again, jolting Amy back out of the dark rabbit hole of self-recriminations and regret she had almost tumbled into. It was a hard kick this time too, and Amy silently thanked God for the distraction. At her last doctor's visit, Amy was told her blood pressure was worryingly high and she needed to lower her stress level. All the more reason to focus on happy thoughts now, despite how much her memories might want to wander.

"You know, Gemma and I met up here when we were kids?" she told Skye. "She's a year older than me. But we did everything together. I don't know if you'll ever have any brothers or sisters. I never did, but I always had Gemma. And she had a younger brother named Ajay."

She was sure she'd told Skye all this before. Amy tended to repeat the same stories. It was hard to keep thinking of lighthearted things to talk about. Not that Gemma's problems with her brother were a happy thought, but it sure was a lot better than thinking about Paul.

"Ajay was my age and he loved adventure books. But Gemma never let him hang out with us, because he was really loud and silly. He would climb on the roof of their cottage and jump out of windows. Once he set off all these fireworks. And then on my fourteenth birthday, he drove my grandma's car into the lake, while my cake was still inside. The police came and the whole party was ruined."

Even though she'd been really upset at the time, it was the kind of memory she laughed about now. But for some reason, Gemma never had. There was a deep-running tension between the sister and brother that Gemma never wanted to talk about. And Amy never wanted to push her to open up about it. She hadn't even known how to contact Ajay when Gemma vanished.

Amy walked into the smaller room where Reepi was bouncing around between the bookshelves, like Amy's own scattered mind. The green-cheeked conure was incredibly good at playing hide-and-seek. She opened the cage door with one hand and stretched out the other to make a landing platform for the bird.

"Come on, Reepi!" she called. "Playtime's over."

There was a flutter of green and gray feathers as the bird glided out from somewhere high above Amy's head and landed on her palm. Dutifully, he began to hop down her arm toward the open cage door.

Suddenly the lights went out, plunging the bookstore into darkness.

Amy's heartbeat quickened, but she took a deep breath and tried to calm it, as her eyes adjusted to the dark. She listened for any sign of trouble. Only silence filled her ears. Okay, so the store had probably blown a fuse or she'd forgotten to pay a utility bill. Gemma had taken her laptop with her when she disappeared, and Amy still hadn't figured out where she kept her bills and files.

She felt Reepi bounce off her arm and then heard the gentle creak of the bird landing on his perch. Amy pulled out her cell phone and used the screen's glow to double-check that Reepi was safely in his cage, then she closed the door and latched it. She put her phone back in her pocket, slid her jacket on and turned to head out the door at the back of the store.

A tall masked man blocked her way. Amy screamed. His cold eyes narrowed through the holes of his ski mask.

She turned and ran toward the front door. Her fingers fumbled for the lock. There was a small canister of bear spray in a pocket inside her jacket, but she wouldn't deploy it until she was outside, in case inhaling the toxic spray hurt Skye.

Strong hands grabbed her from behind. She struggled and kicked back hard against her attacker. He yanked a thick cloth bag over her head, blinding her vision.

"Now you're going to stop fighting," a coarse and heavily accented voice filled her ear, "and you're going to help me find what I'm looking for."

Sergeant Jackson Locke of the RCMP's Ontario K-9 Unit opened the back door of his double-cab pickup truck and watched as his partner, Hudson, leapt inside. The German shepherd promptly lay down on top of Jackson's coat.

"Now what am I going to do if the temperature drops?" Jackson asked. Hudson rested his head on his paws and looked up with big brown eyes. "Just be thankful I've decided that today is not my day. I'm too rattled to interview Amy. We should just pack it in and go find a motel before it gets dark."

For almost three hours, they'd paced laps around the tiny town of Clearwater, as he tried to gear himself up for talking to Amy Scout about his sister's disappearance. Jackson and Hudson had been in the Yukon on an undercover assignment and imbedded in an organized crime ring when his boss, Inspector Ethan Finnick, had slipped him the news that Gemma had gone missing and was presumed dead.

It wasn't until Jackson had closed his Yukon case and gotten back to Ontario last night that he realized just how weak and dicey the evidence was for his sister's disappearance. Nobody had a clue what she'd been doing in the area where her car was found, totaled and empty and submerged in a river. And no one had heard from her since. But the local cops who investigated had no idea how strong, stubborn and downright difficult his older sister could be.

In many ways, he and his sister were polar opposites. But for all their disagreements, he respected the fact that Gemma wasn't the kind of person to give up without a fight.

While the RCMP's Ontario K-9 Unit didn't have official jurisdiction over the investigation into Gemma's disappearance, Finnick had offered Jackson forty-eight hours off work to come up to Clearwater and see what he could find.

What Jackson hadn't been expecting to find was Amy Scout.

Unbidden, Amy's hazel eyes and long honey brown hair filled his mind. For reasons he couldn't begin to guess, it seemed the girl Jackson had a huge crush on—for his entire child-hood and well into his teens—was now all grown up, living alone in his family's cottage, heavily pregnant and even more beautiful than he remembered. Unfortunately, his foolish heart had started beating just as fast at one glimpse of her face as it always had. He felt like a teenager again. Back when he'd known Amy, he'd gone by Ajay—short for "Arthur Jackson." It was a nickname he'd despised but his mother had insisted on because his father was an Arthur too. He'd changed his name to Jackson when he was eighteen.

He was a new man, but he suspected Amy probably hated his guts just as much as she always had.

He hadn't spoken to her since he'd ruined her fourteenth birthday party by hopping into her grandmother's car and crashing it into the lake. He'd been a troubled teen, lashing out after his parents' divorce. At the time, he'd been upset Amy hadn't invited him to her party. And maybe he wanted someone to pay attention to how much he was hurting. He'd tried apologizing to Amy after, but that hadn't gone well.

Jackson ran both hands over his head as if trying to get his brain in gear. He'd parked a little ways from the bookstore in a narrow alley, in the hopes that walking a couple of blocks to the bookstore would help settle his nerves.

It hadn't.

Hudson's shaggy eyebrows rose, as if he knew there had to be a good reason they'd spent five hours driving all the way up from Toronto and it wasn't to just wander around for a bit and leave.

"You're right—I'd better get this over with." He had to go talk to her, whether she still hated him or not. For Gemma.

He wasn't sure if Amy liked dogs—Gemma didn't. Gemma also didn't like cops. Just in case, he was sticking to plain clothes and leaving Hudson behind, at least for now. He rolled the window down, shut the door and then prayed as he jogged down the alley.

Lord, help me be wise. Help me find the right words to say. And help me find my sister.

The back of the bookstore came into view. The door was ajar. At first silence fell. Then he heard a faint and muffled cry. He ran faster. The door flew back on its hinges and he saw them.

A tall man in a dark ski mask had his arm around Amy. He was forcing her backward into the alley. A white cloth bag had been pulled down over Amy's head as a blindfold. She was thrashing against him and fighting for her life. His heart leapt in his chest.

"Stop! Police!" Jackson shouted. "Let her go! Now!"

He ran faster, not even certain they'd heard him

over the sound of the scuffle. Jackson reached for his badge, then realized he'd left it with his gun back in the truck. The masked man dropped Amy and ran. She sank to her knees. Her hand reached inside her jacket as if searching for something.

"Amy!" Jackson shouted. He dropped to the ground beside her and grabbed her by the shoulders, trying to steady her enough to pull the bag off her head. But a fresh scream tore from her lips and she struggled against him. "Hey, it's okay, I'm not going to hurt you—"

But the words had barely left his lips when her right hand darted up in front of his eyes. She was holding a small black canister of bear spray. The ring was wrapped around her finger. The nozzle was pointed directly at his face.

"Stop!" He let her go. "Put that away, it's me, Jackson—"

Amy yanked the pin and fired.

TWO

He had to hand it to her. Amy hadn't even hesitated and her aim was perfect. Two qualities Jackson would've really admired, if it wasn't for the thick stream of noxious chemicals now hitting him right in the face. Immediately his eyes began to burn and stream with tears, blurring his vision. Despite himself, Jackson practically yelped in pain. Amy scrambled back, dropped the canister and began to claw at the hood still covering her face.

"Stop!" he called, only to burst into a heavy coughing fit as the bear spray seared his lungs. "I'm not going to hurt you! I'm a cop!"

She hesitated. "Who are you?"

"Jackson!" He'd told her that. "I work with the RCMP's Ontario K-9 Unit now."

"You're a cop? Why didn't you tell me you're a cop!"

"I did!" he insisted. His voice rose and he nearly choked from the pain. "I'm guessing you didn't hear me. It was kind of chaotic. Now let me walk you away from the blast zone. I'm going to take your hood off but first we're going to move upwind a bit." It felt like fire was filling his lungs with every breath. "Trust me, you don't want to breathe in this stuff. Looks like the blindfold was tied in a knot and you won't be able to reach it."

She paused another moment. Then she turned her head away from the bear spray that still lingered in the air. She let him take her arm and walk her a few feet away from the detonation.

"Who was that guy?" Amy asked.

"I don't know," he admitted.

"He was completely silent," she said. "I didn't even hear him until he was on top of me. Does he have anything to do with what happened to my friend Gemma?" she asked.

"Again, I have no idea," he said. "But I'm here to find out what happened to her."

Amy's head rose defiantly. "I don't believe she's really dead."

"Well, neither do I."

He started coughing again. His lungs and eyes were still stinging, and he could barely see. The first thing he needed to do was rinse his eyes out with water. That would give him temporary but much-needed relief. He'd then have to wash his skin with soap and water, change his clothes too, and see if he could give his eyes an extra rinse with saline solution. It was a whole complicated procedure not made any easier by the inability to properly see and breathe. But he couldn't just leave her there. He wrestled with the knot until it came free. With his help, she pulled the hood off her head. Then she turned around.

Her hazel eyes met his and widened.

"Wow, I got you good," she said. "I'm so sorry about your face. That looks really painful."

Just how bad did he look right now?

"Thanks for your help," she said. "Your name is Jackson, right? I'm Amy. I'll go grab you some water. I've got some in the store."

Wait, didn't she recognize him? It was true they hadn't seen each other in over a decade. He'd lost his youthful chubbiness, bulked up, gotten a new dent in the bridge of his nose thanks to a bad break and grown a beard since then. Not to mention the bear spray was probably doing a number on his features. Then it hit him. In the chaos of the moment, he'd called himself Jackson instead of Ajay. Furious barking filled the air. He turned to see Hudson galloping down the alley toward them. The dog's teeth were bared. Hudson snarled. He must've heard Jackson cry out, managed to wriggle his way through the open truck window and was now charging to Jackson's rescue. Or maybe he'd just smelled the spray and knew it meant trouble.

Amy gasped.

"Hudson, stop!" Jackson ordered. He held up his hand. "Sit. I'm okay. Amy is a friend."

The dog sat promptly. Hudson's head cocked to the side and he whimpered softly.

"Sorry, bud," he added. "I'm sure this stuff smells even worse to you than it does to me." Then he turned to Amy. Her face was pale. "This is my K-9 partner, Hudson."

"Hi, Hudson," Amy said, hesitantly.

The dog thumped his tail in response as if trying to reassure Amy that he hadn't meant to scare her. She turned back to Jackson. "Hang on a second. I'm going to get you some water for your face."

Amy dashed through the open door and was back seconds later with a bottle.

"Thank you." He took it gratefully and splashed it over his eyes. "I should get changed too and wash my skin. Can you help me find somewhere to do that? Then we should sit down and talk about what just happened."

Which was kind of hard to do while it felt like his pores were on fire. The closest motel was over an hour away—the longer he went without changing and washing, the worse it would be for him. He wasn't about to let himself into the family cottage without asking Amy first, even if he did co-own it with his sister. He splashed his eyes again and when he glanced back, Amy was fiddling with her cell phone. Hang on, was she taking his picture?

"Give me a second," she said. "You said your name is Jackson, right? And you're a cop? Here to investigate Gemma Locke's disappearance?"

"That's right."

Amy really did have no idea who he was. But maybe that was a good thing. The police who'd interviewed Amy before had thought she might be hiding something about Gemma's disappearance. In a normal family, the fact he was the missing person's brother would be an advantage, but Amy knew better than anyone that he and Gemma had never been close. The Amy he'd known back when they were teenagers would never have told Gemma's little brother any of her best friend's secrets. Maybe if she didn't know who he was, he'd have an easier time getting her to open up. He could find out the truth...and maybe he'd be less anxious.

"And do you have a last name, Officer Jackson?" Amy asked.

"It's Sergeant Jackson, actually. And my last name is... Finnick."

Before he could think it through, his boss's last name slipped over his tongue.

"Which division?" she pressed.

"The RCMP's Ontario K-9 Unit."

"Do you have a badge?"

"In my truck," he said. "Hudson's got a badge too."

She paused for a moment as if considering his answer. Then she stuck out her hand. He shook it.

"Nice to meet you, Sergeant Jackson Finnick," Amy said. "Sorry again for your face. Now, if you'll excuse me for a minute, I'm just gonna pop back into my store and close everything up for the night. Back in a second."

"I'll come help you," he said.

"No, thanks," Amy said. "You stay out here with Hudson and keep rinsing your eyes."

She walked back into the bookstore.

Jackson looked at Hudson. The dog cocked his head.

"Well, partner, do you think I just made the biggest mistake of my career?"

Amy closed the door almost all the way, leaving it open a crack. Then she calmed her breathing and looked around. The bookstore was eerily quiet now except for the sound of Reepi bouncing happily in his cage. The power was still out but solving that problem would have to wait until tomorrow.

She closed her eyes and prayed.

Thank You, Lord, that I made it out alive.

Please keep me safe now and give me the wisdom I need.

She ran her hands over her belly, feeling for the comforting form of Skye. She held her breath and waited until she felt the flutter of her baby move inside her. Amy exhaled.

Thank You, God.

Skye was okay.

Now, what to do about the intimidatingly handsome Sergeant Jackson and his fierce partner? The cottage was only a few minutes' drive away. He could get cleaned up there and they could talk. She even had a bottle of saline solution for washing out his eyes. But, he was still a total stranger and she didn't know how much she trusted him. Amy glanced down at her sketch pad on the counter. The picture she'd drawn of the man she now knew as Jackson Finnick stared up at her.

Was he really who he said he was? Sure, he'd just told her that there was a badge in his truck, but it could be a fake or even his attempt to lure her to his vehicle. She sighed. Maybe what had happened with Paul had ruined her ability to trust anyone.

She pulled out her cell phone, dialed 911 and told the operator that it was imperative she speak to an officer in the RCMP's Ontario K-9 Unit immediately. There was a click. She waited. And after a long moment, a voice came on the line.

"Constable Caleb Perry, RCMP." The voice was confident and professional. "How can I help you?"

She blinked. "I didn't realize the RCMP had constables."

"Beats calling us entry-level grunts," Caleb said.

"My name is Amy Scout," she said. "I'm calling from Clearwater, Ontario. I have a man here with a large dog who claims to be a K-9 officer with your unit. I wanted to verify his identity."

And get someone to send help right away if he was lying.

"Absolutely," Caleb said. "Though, I can tell you we do have someone in Clearwater at the moment. Is his name Sergeant Locke?"

As in Gemma Locke?

"No." Amy frowned. "Finnick. Sergeant Jackson Finnick. His partner is a German shepherd named Hudson. But Locke is the last name of the person he's here to investigate so maybe there's a mix-up there?"

There was a pause.

"Maybe," Caleb said. His tone was indecipherable.

"I took a picture of them if it helps," she added.

"Yeah, please do send it through," Caleb said. Now he sounded surprised. Or maybe even impressed. "I'll give you my personal cell number you can text it to."

She typed in the number as he rattled it off, then she sent him the picture she'd furtively taken of Jackson and Hudson.

"Yup, that's Jackson Finnick and Hudson all right," he said, after a long moment. "I grabbed some food with Jackson yesterday actually and he told me about the case. They're in Clearwater right now to look into the disappearance of Miss Gemma Locke."

"Yeah," Amy said. So that all checked out. "Gemma was a friend of mine. I'm staying in her cottage and manning her bookstore for her until she gets back."

"So, you don't believe she's dead either," Caleb said, almost as if to himself.

"No, I don't."

"Well, neither does Jackson," Caleb said. "So, you're in good company. Jackson is one of the very best officers I've ever known and Hudson is second to none. If you need more character references, I'm happy to pass the phone around the unit. Everyone will say the same."

"No, that's all right," she said. She was beginning to feel a little foolish. "Thanks so much for your help, officer."

"No problem," Caleb said. "I'll text you the

unit's direct line. Feel free to call either the unit or myself if you need anything."

"I will," she said. "Thank you."

"No problem."

They ended the call. Okay, seemed like there were still some people in the world she could trust.

She found Jackson and Hudson where she'd left them.

"Come on," she said, "grab your bag and I'll take you to the cottage where I'm staying. I've got saline solution and a special soap that's good for getting bear spray off your skin. You can get cleaned up and we can talk about Gemma." She gently grasped his arm. "I'll steer."

"Sounds good," Jackson said.

They made their way to his truck, where he grabbed his jacket and a large bag from the vehicle.

He glanced in the rearview mirror as he did so, clocking his reflection.

"Yup," he said. "I'm a beauty all right."

His eyes were still red and swollen, and his whole face was puffy. Guilt pricked her heart. She couldn't imagine how much pain he was in and yet he hadn't even complained.

As opposed to Paul, who'd lose his temper whenever anyone so much as got his drink order wrong. She would know. When they'd met she'd been a waitress.

"My car's up here," she said brightly. It was a twenty-year-old Volvo with more dings and scrapes than she could count. But it was reliable and it was hers.

Hudson stretched out in the back, Jackson got in the passenger seat, and she started to drive through the woods and down the narrow roads that would lead her back to the cottage.

"So, you have a place up here?" Jackson asked.

"I'm staying at Gemma's, actually," she said. "Making sure everything is taken care of while she's gone."

"I know that you spoke to the local police for their investigation," Jackson said. "But they didn't mention you were living here."

"I hadn't really decided what I was going to do by then."

She still wasn't exactly sure what she was going to do. Skye was due in less than two months and Amy still didn't know what kind of life she could even provide for her.

"How long have you been living at Gemma's?" Jackson asked.

His questions were casual and his tone was light, but she could tell he was interviewing her. She wondered why he'd started by talking about her living situation instead of the attack. Maybe it was his way of easing into the conversation and trying to make her comfortable.

"A few months," she said. "I had some financial problems and she invited me to come live with her."

That was the easiest way to explain it, without going into the wreck Paul had left her life in.

"Where were you before that?" he asked.

"Niagara Falls," she said. "For a little over a year."

"And before that?"

"Traveling the world. I never really settled down anywhere."

Although now that she was about to be a mother, that life was behind her, with nothing left to replace it.

Thick trees pressed in on all sides. Before Paul, her life had been spent leaping from one adventure to the next. She'd just gotten back from backpacking around Europe when she'd taken the waitressing gig in Niagara Falls for a few months to save up for her next adventure. Paul would come in alone and ask for a table in her section. He'd told her he was a real estate developer from Southern California who was visiting on business. She hadn't even found him attractive at first. He was short, balding, and seemed older than the thirty he claimed to be. But she'd thought he was interesting. He'd worn her down slowly over time. There'd been large tips, then dates and gifts, until the next thing she knew she was in a long-distance relationship receiving dozens of calls and texts from him every day.

She frowned at the memory. He'd been so persistent that she never imagined he didn't actually care.

Then he'd surprised her with the most incredible gift of all—blueprints of the tiny seafront art gallery he bought for her. She could fill it with her own sketches and use it to support other up-and-coming talent too. She could hire staff to run it when she traveled. All she had to do was say yes. They'd elope that afternoon and she could start the emigration process immediately. He'd even bought her a ring and booked a wedding chapel in the hopes she'd agree. And impulsively, she decided to jump into the promise of a new adventure.

Only none of it turned out to be real.

He hadn't even lived in California, and she didn't even know his real name. Everything about him was fake.

"Everything okay?" Jackson asked. "You look upset."

A look of genuine concern moved behind his puffy red eyes. Like he actually cared about how she was doing beyond just investigating the case.

"I'm fine," she said. "Just lost in thought."

"Are you okay if we go over the details of what happened back at the bookstore?" he asked. She nodded. "What do you remember about the guy who attacked you?"

"He was tall, masked and, like I said, he was silent." She sighed. "I didn't even hear him until he snuck up on me."

"And you don't have any idea who he was?" Jackson asked. "Could he be an acquaintance or someone you were once in a relationship with?"

"No," she said. "I'm pretty sure I've never met him before."

"Did he say anything to you?"

"Yeah, and he had an accent too."

"What kind of accent?" Jackson asked.

"Australian, I think. Really thick, like he was putting it on."

Jackson nodded. "What did he say?"

"I don't remember the exact words," Amy admitted. "But he told me not to fight and that I was going to help him find something."

"Find what?" Jackson asked.

"I don't know." She shrugged. "But the police never found Gemma's laptop. It wasn't here or in her car, and I'm pretty sure she took it with her."

Jackson's cell phone began to ring. He squinted at the screen. "My eyes are so watery I can't even read it."

She glanced over. "It's Caleb Perry."

He slid his phone back into his pocket. "He's a colleague."

"I know," Amy admitted. "A low-level grunt."

Jackson's eyes widened slightly, then he winced as if it had hurt him to do so. "He's a constable... How did you know that?"

"While I was in the store, I called 911," she went on. "I asked them to patch me into the RC-MP's Ontario K-9 Unit. Maybe I shouldn't have gone through 911, but if you had turned out to be a liar, I would've needed emergency help, now wouldn't I?"

"Yeah," Jackson said. He sounded a bit thrown.

"Caleb answered, and I asked him to verify your identity. I even texted him a picture I'd managed to snap of you and Hudson."

"Wow," Jackson replied. "That's really impressive." There was an odd tone in his voice she couldn't quite place, like he was picking his words very carefully. "What did Caleb say?"

"He verified that you are who you say you are and that you're here looking into what happened to Gemma," she said.

"Did he say anything else?" Jackson asked. He sounded like he was holding his breath.

"Only that you and Hudson are really great."

He exhaled slightly, and Amy wondered what he'd been afraid Caleb might've told her. She turned off the small, rural road onto an even narrower dirt track. The cottage came into view, and beyond it, through the trees, she could see glimpses of the lake. It was a long and meandering body of water that curved through the forest in such a way that no matter where a boat sat on the lake, it was impossible to see all of it at once. Half a dozen islands dotted its surface, most not much larger than a few rocks and trees.

The cottage was two stories. But the second story was a loft, only a third of the size of the bottom floor. It contained two small bedrooms and a landing that jutted out over the living room, which could be reached by a spiral staircase. Most of the cottage consisted of a large living room and kitchen, with a wood-burning stove and floor-to-ceiling windows. She pulled to a stop.

"Welcome to Gemma's cottage," Amy said. "It used to belong to her grandparents, but she bought it from them when she was in college."

Jackson stiffened slightly.

"Actually," he said, "the way I heard it, Gemma and her brother jointly bought it from their grandparents."

"Huh, I didn't know that," Amy said. It looked like Jackson really had done his homework. "I've never seen him up here."

"I take it he's busy with work," Jackson said. There was that odd tone in his voice again.

She pulled to a stop by the back door.

"Do you know if anyone questioned him about what happened to Gemma?" she asked. "Because wherever she was going that day, it was important to her and she didn't want to talk about it. Maybe he had a financial motive, if she was living in a cottage they jointly owned, or he was in some kind of trouble."

As much as she hated to think it.

"Oh, police have talked to him," Jackson said. "But do you suspect him? Do you think there's something wrong with the guy?"

"No," Amy said. "Not really. But Ajay was into some really stupid petty stuff when he was younger. Pranks, trespassing, that kind of thing. Maybe he went downhill and got involved in even worse stuff since then."

Jackson didn't answer. They got out of the car and started for the cottage.

"Would you mind if we let Hudson chill outside on the front porch?" Amy asked. "Gemma isn't a fan of dogs in the house, and he's a pretty big guy."

Not to mention, he'd seemed downright terrifying when he'd been charging toward her back at the store, despite how sweet his shaggy face was now as he looked up at her.

"I'm happy to put out a bowl of water and a blanket for him," she added. "But I don't know if I left out things he might eat or things he could knock over. I wasn't expecting—"

"It's okay," Jackson said, cutting her off. "It's fine. The weather's clear and it's a nice temperature out for a dog with a coat like his. He won't mind."

"Thank you," she said, feeling truly grateful at how quickly Jackson had agreed.

They walked around the side of the cottage to the front porch that looked out over the lake. Thick trees ringed them on all sides, hiding their neighboring cottages, all of which were empty this time of year. They left Hudson on the front porch then walked through the sliding glass door into the main room. Amy found Jackson the soap, saline and a towel then pointed him toward the washroom.

She busied herself with tidying up. Enough chicken stew for six people bubbled gently in a Crock-Pot on the kitchen counter. She turned off the heat to let it cool enough to eat. Amy had left her charcoal pencils, sketch pads and pictures scattered around the room. She arranged them into a single neat pile on the dining room table.

Her stomach rumbled. Skye was hungry and didn't want to wait. She walked back into the kitchen and pulled out a box of crackers, a jar of peanut butter and a knife. Amy spread a dab of peanut butter on the first cracker, popped it straight into her mouth without pausing to put it on a plate, and then did the same with the second. She was about a dozen crackers in when she realized Jackson was standing in the bathroom doorway in a fresh, clean blue shirt, watching her. She blushed, realizing he'd just caught her snacking.

"How are you feeling?" she asked. "You're looking better."

Some of the redness and swelling had subsided. She noticed for the first time that his eyes were green, reminding her of Gemma.

Her missing friend had green eyes too. Not pseudo-green, like Amy's hazel ones, but the kind of bright green that silently caught a person's attention from across the room.

"I feel better," he said. "Do you have enough crackers for two?"

"I actually have chicken stew if you're hungry," she said. "There's plenty if you want to stay for dinner. It's a lot better than crackers, I just couldn't wait until it cooled. Pregnancy hunger isn't like any other form of pangs I've ever experienced. There's something that feels really urgent about it. Do you have any kids?"

"No," Jackson said. He walked over to the couch. "Never married, no family and no kids. It's just me and Hudson. I'm not really cut out for the parent life." He chuckled sadly as he sat, and something in his tone made her suspect there was a story there. "Is this kid your first?"

"Yup." She put the peanut butter and crackers away. Then she got out bowls for stew.

"Do you need a hand with that?" he called.

"No," she said. "I'm good."

"How far along are you in the pregnancy?" he asked.

"Almost thirty-four weeks," she said.

"Do you know if you're having a boy or a girl yet?"

"A girl." She smiled. "I call her Skye."

"I like it," he said. "And you moved in with Gemma after you were pregnant?"

"Yeah." Now his steady string of questions was beginning to feel more like an interrogation. She guessed Jackson wasn't one for meaningless small talk. Steam rose off the stew as she lifted the lid. She stirred it slowly, letting the warm aroma fill the room. "But I moved in before I knew I was pregnant. My so-called husband left me before either of us knew I had a baby on the way. We were only married a couple of weeks actually."

"Wow, I'm sorry," Jackson said.

"Don't be. I'm better off without him."

The morning she'd gotten home from buying groceries to find Paul gone, all she knew for certain was that his cell phone had been disconnected, the eight thousand dollars she'd had in savings had been drained from her bank account and he'd taken every expensive gift he'd ever bought her. It was only due to Gemma's internet sleuthing afterward that she'd found out Paul had at least three different names he used, several children by multiple women, a wife in Michigan and another in Wyoming.

What he didn't have was an art studio.

Getting the marriage annulled had been a snap. Getting any form of justice had been another matter entirely. Turned out Canadian law enforcement wasn't about to dedicate a lot of resources to scouring the United States for a man whose real name and location she didn't even know over the theft of a few thousand dollars.

Amy scooped large ladles full of chicken, potatoes and vegetables into bowls. Then she walked over and handed one to Jackson. He stayed on the couch, while she sat in the rocking chair, and they talked about Gemma. Amy went over everything she knew about the days before Gemma's disappearance and where she could have been going, which wasn't much.

"It goes without saying that I searched every inch of both the bookstore and this place for clues in the days after Gemma left," Amy said. "Of course, the police searched too. So, whatever the intruder was looking for, I don't think he's going to find it." She stirred her stew slowly and watched as steam rose from her bowl. "At this point I'm wondering if I should start checking every book in the place for hidden messages. But there are thousands of them."

"The police who interviewed you indicated they thought you weren't being fully honest with them," Jackson said.

"Really?" She felt her eyebrows rise. Was this why Jackson was grilling her? "Well, I told them everything I know. I can't tell them what I don't know."

"How was the bookstore doing?" Jackson asked.

"Good," Amy said. "I think."

"Was anything upsetting Gemma?" Jackson asked. "Was there anything out of the ordinary going on?"

"I don't know." Amy frowned and pushed the stew around in her bowl. "She was working incredibly long hours. Gemma used to talk about going back to school or making a career change. But since I moved in, she's been really focused on being at the store. Sometimes she'd be there until after midnight and then right back there in the morning. But I have no idea why."

She'd wondered if Gemma had been continuing to look into Paul, even though Amy had asked her to drop it.

"Gemma was always a very private person," Amy said. "She was the kind who'd avoid conflict at all costs."

She blew out a breath.

"My doctor has been worried about my blood pressure and told me to keep my stress levels low," she added. "Knowing Gemma, she'd have thought twice before telling me anything that might've upset me."

Jackson nodded. "Where did she tell you she was going the day she disappeared?"

"She didn't," Amy said. "She just told me she needed to run an errand and asked me to manage the bookstore while she was gone. That was the last I heard from her." She set her bowl on the coffee table. She'd suddenly lost her appetite. "I just keep wishing I'd asked her what was going on."

Jackson put his bowl down beside hers. His fingers brushed her hand and then squeezed reassuringly for a moment before letting go. There was something about the simple gesture that sent tears rushing to her eyes.

"None of this is your fault," Jackson said. "You hear me? You can't blame yourself for any of this. Now, I'm going to take Hudson to the closest dog-friendly motel for the night, then come back here in the morning and see what we can find. It'll be okay. I promise."

His phone began to ring again. This time she couldn't see the name when he checked the screen. But whoever was calling, Jackson's face paled slightly.

"I'm going to take this outside," he said. "Give me a second."

He walked out the front door with the still-ringing phone in his hand and closed the door behind him. He signaled Hudson, and the two of them walked around the side of the building and still the phone rang. Seemed he was waiting until he was completely out of earshot before answering it.

The sun was beginning to set over the lake in shades of pink and purple fading down to a deep royal blue. This place was so beautiful and peaceful. For years it had been her favorite place on the planet. It was hard to think of anything bad happening here.

Something moved in the trees to her right. She turned quickly. But all she could see was an indistinct blur disappearing into the night. Had someone been there? Was her imagination playing tricks on her or was someone watching the cabin?

THREE

Jackson stared at his ringing cell phone as if it were a hand grenade about to explode.

Inspector Ethan Finnick, head of the RCMP's Ontario K-9 Unit and Jackson's boss, was calling. No doubt to ask what Jackson had been thinking using Finnick's own last name for an impromptu cover identity. Jackson had never imagined that Amy would immediately try to verify that he was who he said he was. Clearly he'd underestimated her, in more ways than one. He'd been beyond relieved when Caleb had covered for him. Caleb was a good friend and an outstanding officer who'd only recently transferred into the K-9 unit and still hadn't been assigned a partner.

He didn't expect Finnick to be equally as understanding.

"Jackson!" Amy called.

He declined the phone call, stuck the phone in his pocket and turned to see her running around the side of the cottage.

"Is everything okay?" he asked.

"I don't know," she said and gasped a breath. "I think I saw someone in the bushes, but I can't be sure."

Jackson signaled Hudson, and together they ran back around the side of the building. He scanned the darkness but couldn't see anything.

"Where did you see him?" Jackson asked.

"There." Amy pointed to a gap in the trees a few feet from the water.

"Get inside the cottage," Jackson said. "Keep the door locked and your phone in your hand. I'll be back in a moment."

He waited until Amy was safely inside, then together he and Hudson ran in the direction she'd pointed. They burst through the trees. There was no one there and yet multiple sets of footprints marred the ground in indistinct and overlapping shapes, some more faded than others. Someone had definitely been there in the past and not just once, but he couldn't tell how long ago.

Had they been watching Amy, Gemma or both of them?

He instructed Hudson to search. While the dog seemed to pick up a scent, he lost it again a few feet later at the water's edge. Frustration burned the back of Jackson's throat and he channeled it into prayer.

Lord, help me figure out what's going on and

catch whoever's behind this. Help me keep Amy safe and find my sister. He took a deep breath and let it out slowly. *And whatever I face, through all of this help me be kind, wise and the type of person I want to be.*

He and Hudson went back to the cottage, where he found Amy waiting for them just inside the door.

"I'm kind of hoping you're going to tell me there was nobody there and I was imagining everything," Amy said.

"Sadly, I think someone has been watching the cottage," Jackson said. "I just don't know how recently."

Worry flooded Amy's eyes. He watched as her arms wrapped around her belly as if trying to cradle her unborn child and keep her safe.

"Change of plans," Jackson said. "I'm going to stay in Clearwater tonight, so I'm close by if you need me. It doesn't feel right leaving you here alone until we find out more about what's going on. I'll sleep in my truck."

"There's a camper parked around the far side of the cottage," she said. "You're welcome to stay there. It's probably twenty years old, but it'll keep you both dry."

He almost smirked. Yes, he knew the old camper very well. He'd practically lived in it all summer long when he was a kid and wouldn't be surprised if he found dog-eared copies of his old adventure books hidden behind the cushions. He fed Hudson dinner and they walked him together. Then they returned to the cottage, where Amy and Jackson shared another bowl of stew and some homemade cookies. All the while, his phone kept buzzing in his pocket like an angry mosquito, until he eventually muted the ringer.

Jackson knew he'd have to call Finnick back eventually. But for now he was putting it off. There was something just so easy and comfortable about talking with Amy that made it hard to walk away from her. She had the most incredible laugh—it wasn't just pretty but generous too, and it made his own lips turn up in a smile. He couldn't remember ever having seen her art when they were younger, but now every corner of the cottage seemed alive with vibrant lines, shapes and colors. Besides, the longer they talked, the greater the possibility she might remember something important about Gemma. He didn't just enjoy her company; she was a vital part of finding his sister.

Or so he kept telling himself.

The sun set completely, leaving nothing but an inky black sky with an almost-full moon hanging high above them. Amy drove Jackson and Hudson back to the place where he'd left his pickup truck so he could retrieve it. Then they came back to the cottage and wished each other a good night. Jackson hauled his gear, a sleeping bag and a blanket for Hudson through the trees to the old camper.

He was a little surprised that Gemma had never suggested removing it, and wondered if she'd kept it up as some kind of olive branch because she knew how much it meant to him. It was cleaner than expected, with no leaks and few cobwebs. The ceiling was lower than he remembered. But the smell of canvas surrounding him was just the same as always. He unfurled his sleeping bag on one of the bunks, hopped up and sat there leaning back against the wall. Hudson leapt up beside him and lay his large, furry head on his knees. Jackson stroked the soft fur between his partner's ears.

"Thank you for being so patient with Amy today," he said. "I hope you didn't mind chilling outside. You're a really good dog and I'm sure she'll see that too."

Finally, he turned to his phone and called Finnick. His boss answered on the second ring.

"Finnick here."

"Hi, it's Jackson," he said. "I'm so sorry for not calling you back sooner and I know we have to talk. But I was with Amy. Somebody tried to kidnap her."

Finnick inhaled sharply. "This would be Amy Scout? Your sister's roommate?"

"Yeah," Jackson said, "and best friend since childhood."

"Is she all right?" Finnick asked.

"A little shaken," Jackson said, "but fine. She's one of the strongest women I've ever met. She bear sprayed me when I rushed to the rescue, thinking I might be working with the guy who attacked her. Got me right in the eyes."

Finnick snorted. Seemed he was Team Amy on that one. So was he. Jackson quickly ran his boss through the kidnapping incident at the bookstore and the evidence that someone might have been watching the cottage for days, or even weeks. Finnick was an incredible officer, and Jackson was thankful that no matter how confounded he might be by what Jackson had done in borrowing his name, Finnick's top priority was still making sure the civilian was safe. Jackson had never met an officer who was more dedicated to making sure victims and their families got the justice and closure they deserved. More times than Jackson could count, as he was packing up for the day, he'd glance into Finnick's office and see his boss still sitting at his desk, with his K-9 partner Nippy curled up at his feet, poring over cold cases with such intense focus it was like Finnick took the fact each one was still unsolved personally.

"Amy's very pregnant," Jackson said. "Late third trimester. As much as I appreciate everything she's done to help keep Gemma's store running in her absence, I don't feel safe leaving her up here alone."

"Neither do I." Finnick blew out a breath. "All right, this is where jurisdictions get tricky. Because I can't just easily step in as a head of the RCMP's Ontario K-9 Unit and wrangle a case out of the hands of the local police who are heading the investigation into Gemma's disappearance—"

"Even if they've bungled it and let it die?" Jackson interjected.

"Even if they've made a dog's breakfast of it," Finnick said. "But I can definitely open an investigation into the attack on Amy and ask local police for their files to help in our investigation."

A wry determination moved through his boss's voice. It was reassuring. Jackson closed his eyes for a moment and thanked God that Finnick had given him a couple of days off work to look into his sister's disappearance on his own and that he sounded willing to throw resources behind helping Amy.

"Now, the only description we have of her attacker is that he's tall, moved silently and has an Australian accent?" Finnick confirmed.

"Correct," Jackson said. He opened his eyes. "Amy thinks the accent might be fake. Like I mentioned, I suspect someone has been watching the cottage for a while. I don't know why she was attacked today or what that has to do with what happened to Gemma. All I can think is that the investigation into my sister's disappearance had been fairly dormant until I got back yesterday and started pulling on every thread I could find. I might've attracted someone's attention."

"I'd agree with that," Finnick said. "They'd practically closed the case until you started kicking up a fuss."

"Maybe I rattled whoever's behind this," Jackson said, "and they decided they had to act fast."

"It's a definite possibility," Finnick said. "Any new leads on what happened to your sister?"

"Not yet," Jackson said. "By the sound of things, Gemma was spending very long hours at the bookstore in the weeks before she disappeared, but we still have no idea what she was doing in South River. It's in between here and Huntsville, so maybe that's where she was really headed. Amy thinks she was hiding something, but she doesn't know what."

"And you're convinced that local police are wrong and she's still alive?" Finnick asked.

"I am," Jackson said. He had to be. He couldn't afford to think anything else or the grief would overwhelm him. "Gemma is the most tenacious and relentless person I know. She's a lot more introverted than me. We butted heads constantly as kids, because I was really outgoing and she was conflict avoidant. But if anyone could survive a hit job, it's her."

Despite their differences, she'd always looked out for him in her own way. Like how she'd never been a fan of cops after Jackson had encountered a couple of truly terrible ones. This was when he'd ended up in a special program for kids with behavioral problems, after the whole car incident. It was ironic. Gemma was so protective she couldn't get over the fact he'd forgiven the cops who'd mistreated him and even joined their ranks.

"Well, I hope you're right," Finnick said. "Now, to face the elephant in the room. What I don't understand is why, faced with all this, you then decided to lie to Amy Scout about your identity? Or how you thought it would help anything in regards to this investigation?"

The fact that Jackson had been anticipating the question didn't stop it from stinging. He'd worked on almost a dozen undercover operations in his career, both large and small, and never once had he been accused of lying, especially not by a superior officer.

"The officer who'd interviewed Amy initially about Gemma's disappearance wondered if Amy was hiding something," Jackson said. "I have an unfortunate history with this witness, and I didn't want that to get in the way of finding out what she knew. So, when I realized she didn't recognize me, rather than dredging up the past and risking the investigation, I made the split-second call to turn this into an undercover operation."

"But that's not what we do." Finnick's tone was so sharp it could've cut straight through the flimsy canvas walls surrounding him. "You know better than most that we spend days preparing for undercover work. I will not have my officers running around whipping up new identities willy-nilly on the fly. Did you even put an ounce of thought into your cover story?"

"No," Jackson admitted.

"Great, so you're winging it," Finnick said, and Jackson could practically hear him rolling his eyes.

"I know. I need to take a breath and figure out my cover before it comes back to bite me," Jackson said. Then again, if he managed to keep Amy at arm's length he wouldn't have to. There was no need to let things get personal between them, any more than they already had.

"Ha," Finnick said. "It's going to bite you either way at this point. What you need to do is apologize and tell her the truth as soon as possible. What exactly is your history with Amy Scout?"

He paused. "It's personal."

"Not if it has the potential to impact both an attempted kidnapping and a missing person's case," Finnick said. "And I have the authority to pull you back into the office and dispatch another officer to apologize to her for what you've done."

"Okay, truth is, I was a real idiot back when she knew me," Jackson said, quickly. "I was obnoxious. I had a lot of energy and a lot of pain over my parents' divorce, and rather than channeling that in a healthy way I pulled a lot of stupid pranks, which eventually landed me in a program for kids with problems, and that saved my life and got me on the right track. But before that, when I was fourteen, I took a joyride in her grandmother's car because I was upset Amy hadn't invited me to her birthday party. I crashed right down the hill, practically through the party, hit a couple of tables and ended up in the lake. Thankfully, nobody was hurt."

Finnick didn't say anything. The silence on the other end of the phone was almost deafening.

"A year later, I wrote her a letter," Jackson went on, "as part of my therapy process. I was supposed to make amends to people I hurt. I apologized for what I'd done, and what I'd been like back then. I also admitted I had a crush on her and had acted really immaturely when she didn't invite me to her party."

"And did she respond?" Finnick asked.

"She sent my letter back with big block letters

printed across it saying she never wanted to see me again," Jackson said. "She said she hated me. And she had every reason to."

"Such teenage dramatics," Finnick said, under his breath. "Both of you."

"The issue is that I'm genuinely embarrassed and ashamed about the person I used to be," Jackson added. Even now, when Amy asked him if he had a family, he couldn't help but think that he'd mess up any kids he had so badly they'd end up behaving even worse than he had. "My sister and I were never close, while Gemma and Amy have always been joined at the hip. I was afraid if Amy remembered me, she'd shut up tighter than a clam and refuse to speak to me." He clasped the back of his neck. "She even suggested that I could be the one who'd done something terrible to Gemma. She practically implied I murdered her for her share of the cottage."

"And you thought if she knew that you were Gemma's brother, you wouldn't get the information you needed to figure out what happened to your sister," Finnick said.

"Pretty much," Jackson said, "especially considering she was already terrified from having almost been kidnapped and had just bear sprayed me. But I take it you think I made the wrong call."

"Probably," Finnick replied. "But I also think

that at this point we're stuck with the situation you've made for yourself, at least until tomorrow. But, as you know, due to a problem with our usual dog breeder, I have a couple of incredible new constables in our unit who don't yet have dogs to continue their training with. So, I'm going to get constables Caleb Perry and Blake Murphy to help you on this. You've already roped Caleb in, and Blake has a wonderful knack for dealing with challenging cases. Expect them to make contact with you in the morning and to meet up with you in Clearwater by early afternoon."

Which also meant they'd be able to take over the case and help deal with the fallout if Amy wanted nothing more to do with him once he told her the truth.

"Understood," Jackson said.

"I have to admit, I'm surprised you've pulled it off so long," Finnick said. "I would've imagined the cottage was full of family pictures of you."

"We're not that kind of family," Jackson said, feeling a twinge of regret. "My parents' divorce was really toxic. And I guess neither Gemma nor I had any great desire to remember our child-hood."

Or repeat it with families of their own. At least, he didn't.

"Out of curiosity, why do you think Amy hasn't recognized you yet?" Finnick asked.

"I didn't spend a lot of time up close with Amy when we were kids," Jackson said. "I was a chubby kid then. I've gotten more lean and added more muscle. I've broken my nose since I saw her last. Plus, I've grown a beard."

But the fact Finnick had used the word *yet* hung in the back of his mind like a flashing warning sign.

"One more thing," Finnick said. A warmer tone moved through his voice, which suddenly reminded Jackson that the seasoned officer was almost old enough to be his father. "We all made mistakes when we were younger that we've spent the rest of our lives kicking ourselves for. The wise ones among us learn to face up to those mistakes and learn from them. You're a good officer, Jackson. Don't let the mistakes you made over a decade ago jeopardize this case or your career."

Jackson looked up at the plastic roof above his head. That was easier said than done.

Night came early for Amy like a heavy blanket, dragging her down into unconsciousness before she'd even had time to ask herself what she thought about the handsome man and protective dog who were keeping guard nearby in the camper.

But it seemed her initially peaceful sleep was too good to last. Her body was jolted awake shortly after one o'clock in the morning by the feeling of Skye kicking inside her. The small baby's kicks were urgent and relentless, as if her unborn child sensed that something was wrong and was trying to get her attention. And for the first time since the terrifying incident back at the bookstore, Amy could feel the full extent of her fear seeping into her veins. Her shoulders began to shake as if the temperature had dropped. She took in a long calming breath. Then Amy pressed her hand against her belly, feeling Skye's tiny foot against her palm.

"Hey, it's okay," she said. "I'm awake. What do you need? Are you hungry? Or do you just randomly feel like doing jazz aerobics right now?"

She closed her eyes to pray and felt her lungs tighten in her chest. It seemed the fear wasn't about to leave her so easily.

Lord, I need Your help. I don't feel safe staying here alone at the cottage. But I don't really have anywhere else to go. All I want is to keep Skye safe, but I don't know how, let alone who's after me or why. Am I being foolish by holding onto the hope that Gemma's still alive out there somewhere and everything's going to be okay?

She opened her eyes and looked out the window at the dark woods, searching for the shape of the camper. There'd been something comforting, almost peaceful, about sitting with Jackson in the living room talking earlier. He hadn't once snapped at her or made her feel bad about hitting him with the bear spray. And he seemed to really listen when she talked and paid attention to what she was saying. It was different from what she was used to. But it was nice. It made her feel relaxed and safe, in a way nobody ever had before. Being with Paul had felt like riding a roller coaster. And as much as she loved Gemma, lately her friend had a tension to her, as if she'd been battling some unknown enemy just outside Amy's view.

Being with Jackson felt like stepping outside into the sunshine on a warm day.

"I'm not sure how to tell you this," Amy said out loud to Skye, "but before I saw your tiny little shape on a sonogram, I never wanted a permanent home or a family. I was spontaneous, and I liked it that way. Even with Paul, I was lured in by the fact it was a long-distance relationship and he traveled a lot. You're not even here yet and already you feel like the first thing in my life that has ever been permanent."

And what would her life be now? She had no idea. All she knew was that it would be nothing like it'd ever been before.

A crash sounded in the cottage below her, like someone had accidentally knocked her haphazard pile of sketch pads off the table. Had Jackson let himself back into the cottage for a drink of water or something? Was he struggling to find the light switch?

She swung her feet over the edge of the bed, slid her arms through her housecoat and belted it over her long flannel pajamas. Then she crept in her stocking feet to her bedroom door, opened it a crack and peered out. She looked down, past the railing of the landing at the main floor below. The living room lay dark and empty beneath her. Silence had fallen again. The cottage was so quiet that if someone was there, she couldn't even hear them breathing. Then slowly shapes began to form in the dim gray light that filtered in through the windows, and she saw him.

A tall, masked figure was climbing up the spiral stairs toward her.

Amy closed her bedroom door softly and locked it behind her. The man who'd kidnapped her was inside her cottage, coming down the hall toward her. She ran for the window and threw it open.

"Jackson!" She shouted his name into the night. "Help! The intruder is here! He's in the cottage!"

And the intruder, whoever he was, had definitely heard her now. But had Jackson? There was no reply from him, just the rustling of leaves in the darkness. Was he there? Had he heard her? Was he even now creeping quietly through the trees to her rescue?

I don't even know if I can trust him.

Or maybe something had happened to Jackson, like something had happened to Gemma.

She couldn't hear the intruder either. Was he in the next room? Was he just outside her door? If he hadn't knocked over her books, she might never have heard him. She ran her hand over her belly.

"Thank you for waking me up," she whispered to Skye.

But now what?

She heard the soft telltale squeak of Gemma's door opening on its hinges. Maybe the intruder was searching her room. But what was he looking for? Moments later she heard Gemma's door close again and knew the intruder was on his way to her room. The balcony was so narrow and the spiral staircase down to the main floor was so steep that she couldn't risk making a run for it. Not with a criminal out there who might try to force her over the edge or kidnap her again. She looked out the window again. Tree branches rustled beneath her. Was that Jackson and Hudson? Had he heard her calling out to him for help? Were they on their way?

Help me, Lord, I'm trapped! Am I foolish to hold onto the hope that they're coming for me?

She looked out the window, feeling the mounting fear rise inside her. Then she looked back over her shoulder at the bedroom door. She couldn't stay hidden in here forever. But there was a sloping overhang about three feet beneath her. The room had once belonged to Ajay and when they'd been kids, he used to climb out the window, across the overhang, and leap down onto the water barrels, especially whenever he'd been grounded. She'd only done it once, when he'd been teasing her and Gemma about being too scared to try it.

Well, now she was far more afraid of whoever was on the other side of the door.

A faint rattling sounded from behind her, as if someone was trying to pick the lock.

She slid her body through the window one leg at a time until she was sitting on the window ledge staring out at the night. Was she really going to do this? What other choice did she have?

Her breath tightened in her chest. The doorknob turned behind her. Her bedroom door creaked open. She caught one fleeting glimpse of the same masked assailant stepping in through her bedroom door.

Then she pushed off from the windowsill and let her body drop down onto the slanted roof below. It was steeper than she remembered. She slid toward the edge, prayers spilling from her lips as she desperately grabbed at the shingles, trying to slow her descent. Then her stockinged feet hit the rain gutter, stopping her with a jolt and almost pitching her forward over the edge. Instead, the gutter held firm.

Thank You, Lord.

Something rustled in the trees, but she didn't risk leaning forward to see what it was. Instead, Amy began to shimmy her way along the roof, moving sideways like a crab. But her socks didn't give her much grip. The shingles were loose under her hands.

A light flickered on and off in the forest so quickly that she couldn't tell where it was coming from.

"Amy?" Jackson's whisper was faint in the darkness.

"Jackson?" she whispered back. "I shouted for you."

"I heard. I didn't want to tip anyone off that I was here."

Well, she'd have liked the heads-up he was coming to her rescue.

"Where are you?" he asked.

"Here."

"Where?"

"On the roof."

"You're what?" His voice rose slightly. "Never mind. Hang on and don't move. I'm coming."

She could hear the intruder moving through her room behind her. What if he had a weapon? Or got to her before Jackson did? Should she just wait there for Jackson to rescue her? Or keep climbing down?

Suddenly the decision was out of her hands as she felt the tiles rip loose beneath her fingers. She scrambled in vain for another handhold, but it was too late. The gutter broke free. Amy screamed as suddenly she tumbled forward, off the steep roof and into the darkness below.

FOUR

Lord, please protect my child! The desperate prayer filled her heart as—for what felt like an excruciating and terrifying moment—Amy felt herself falling through the air. Then she landed against a sturdy chest. Strong arms tightened gently around her and she realized he must've run for her.

"It's okay," Jackson's voice soothed in her ear. "I'm here. I've got you. What were you even doing up there?"

"The intruder…was in…my room." Her breaths were coming out so sharp and shallow, she could barely speak. "He's looking… He's looking for something."

Quickly, Jackson stepped under the cover of the porch and out of the view of anyone looking out the window. His arms tightened around her. "Are you all right? Did he hurt you?"

"I'm fine. He didn't see me." She tried to pull in a deeper breath. "It's no big deal. Gemma's brother used to jump off the roof all the time when we were kids."

"You're not him," Jackson said. "Are you sure you're okay?"

No, she wasn't. But her heart was racing in her chest and she had to slow it down, for Skye's sake.

"I need to lie down," she admitted, "and slow my heart rate."

"We need to get you out of here in case he comes looking for you," Jacskon said. "I'll take you to the camper. Hudson will guard you while I go see if I can catch the intruder."

"But Hudson is just a dog."

"Trust me." Jackson's voice was firm and un-relenting. "He's also an RCMP officer and he'll protect you."

He turned and started carrying her swiftly through the trees toward the camper. Hudson ran alongside them.

"I know you and Hudson didn't get off to the best start," he added. "But I promise he'll keep you safe. If anyone comes within a mile of you, he'll bark his head off. His hearing is far better than ours." He blew out a breath. "And if anyone tries to step foot near the camper, it will not go well for them."

When they reached the trailer, he opened the door and gently set her down just inside the doorway. A faint orange light flickered on above a bunk to her right. She crawled onto the bed, lay down and pressed her hands flat against the mattress, willing her racing heart to slow its rapid pace. Skye was kicking so frantically, Amy almost doubled over.

"The light will flicker off when I close the door," Jackson said. "But there's a flashlight with a dimmer in the side pocket. There's a folding knife in there too, not that Hudson will let anyone get within striking distance of you."

He turned to Hudson and directed the German shepherd to jump inside and sit in front of Amy, facing the door.

"Guard Amy," Jackson said, firmly. "Keep her safe."

Hudson woofed softly.

Jackson turned to Amy. "What am I walking into?"

"Same guy as before," she said.

"Did you see him?"

"Yeah," she said. "Really well. He's tall and masked. He was clearly searching the cabin for something."

"Did he have a weapon?" he asked.

"Not that I saw."

Jackson nodded. "Okay."

Still, Jackson hesitated in the doorway, as if uncertain whether to leave her or not. She didn't want him to go.

Lord, I feel safe with him here. And now he's walking into danger. Please protect him and keep him safe. Keep us both safe.

"You should go," Amy said. "Catch whoever is behind this before he finds whatever he's after and gets away with it."

"Yes, ma'am," Jackson said. She could hear his smile in the darkness.

He turned the lock on the handle and then closed the door. The orange light flickered out. She lay there for a moment listening for the sound of Jackson moving away through the woods.

Hudson glanced toward her and woofed softly as if trying to reassure her. She reached down and ran her hand along his back, feeling the warmth of his soft fur beneath her fingers. Hudson licked her fingers in response. Then he turned his attention back to the door. The dog's ears perked, listening for any sound in the darkness.

She closed her eyes and forced her breathing to slow.

God, I feel as if the world is shifting beneath my feet.

She'd liked living a spontaneous life. It had been fun, like she'd been on a raft exploring one fast-paced river after the next. But now, it was as if her tiny raft had been swept out onto the huge and wild ocean. She was beaten down by torrential rains. And every time she thought for a moment she'd begun to find her footing, another wave would come and knock her down.

I want my best friend Gemma back, Lord. I can't imagine her being dead, and I want so very much for the police to find her alive. I want Jackson to catch whoever is stalking me and for the nightmare I'm living in to stop. Above all, I want a break from the chaos.

I need peace. Please, bring Your strong and lasting peace into my life.

Finally, she felt her breathing begin to slow, and Skye settled within her.

Thank You, God.

She reached inside the camper's side storage flap, for the flashlight Jackson told her was stashed there. Instead, she felt something rectangular. It was soft around the edges. She pulled it out and ran her fingers along it.

It was a book and there was a piece of paper tucked between the pages.

Glad for the distraction, she dipped her hand back into the pocket again and felt around until she finally found the flashlight. Then she pulled a blanket over her head, just like when she and Gemma had been kids trying not to get caught reading after dark.

She flicked the light on. It was one of Ajay's old adventure novels, about two brothers who explored incredible places solving crimes. She pulled out the piece of paper. It was ragged at the side like it had been ripped from a spiral notebook. Words were scrawled across the page in large bold letters, only to be dramatically scratched out as if someone had tried to erase any evidence that they'd ever been written.

Hi Amy,
I like you. Do you like me?

Yo Amy,
I think you're amazing. Do you want to be my girlfriend? Yes or No.

Dear Amy,
Do you like pizza? Want to go get some in town maybe?

Her heart stopped in her chest. She'd discovered something she wasn't supposed to see. Ajay had had a crush on her. But she'd had no idea, and he'd never sent her a letter like this. But he'd tried to write one…she guessed when they were about thirteen, judging by the handwriting. Had Gemma known? And if Ajay felt this way, why had he never told her?

Jackson pressed his body against the living room wall of his cottage and listened. He could hear the sound of the clock ticking and his own breath rising and falling. Trees rustled somewhere beyond the cottage walls. A cold breeze cut through the air. The door to the front porch had been left open.

Did that mean the intruder was already gone? Had he found what he was looking for and escaped while Jackson was taking care of Amy? Or was he still hiding somewhere in the darkness?

Jackson crept through the main room with his gun drawn. Every nerve in his body was on high alert with the knowledge that at any moment he could be ambushed by an unseen enemy. Slowly, his eyes began to adjust to the light filtering in through the large picture windows. Thankfully the open concept cottage didn't provide too many spaces for someone to hide. He missed having his K-9 partner there beside him. If Hudson had been there, he'd know in an instant whether or not they were really alone.

He looked around the main floor. It was hard to even tell for sure that anyone had been in the cottage. But he was certain that drawers and cupboards had been opened and rummaged through. Books had been rearranged on the shelves. Twice now, Amy had told him that the intruder usually moved silently. Seemed like he also knew how to avoid leaving a trace.

Who was this man? What did he want?

Why was he after Amy?

Jackson was grateful he'd gotten to her in time. Suddenly, the memory of holding Amy in his arms as he ran to the camper filled his mind. She'd been shaking and obviously terrified. Yet, at the same time he was amazed by how incredibly brave and courageous she'd been. Climbing out the window, like he used to do when he was a kid, was a pretty gutsy move. It also might've saved her life.

Jackson shuddered to think what could've happened if she hadn't woken up and escaped, and he silently thanked God for protecting her.

He'd always liked Amy. She'd been cute, smart, spontaneous and fun as a teen. But since reconnecting with her, he could see just how strong and caring she was too. The way Amy had taken on running Gemma's store without missing a beat was incredible, especially considering her own circumstances. He needed to find out what had happened to Gemma. Not just because he loved his sister and had to know she was okay. But because he needed to give Amy closure too and try to bring her best friend home.

Jackson finished his sweep of the main floor. Slowly he crossed to the spiral staircase guided by the dim light, the feeling in his gut and the faith that God would watch over him. He planted a foot on the first step. It creaked underneath his weight.

Suddenly, a shadow moved across the balcony above him. Then, before Jackson could even blink, a figured leaped over the railing and hurtled down toward him.

Instinctively, Jackson raised his weapon to fire. But it was too late—the taller man landed on top of him, knocking Jackson to the floor in a full-body blow. Jackson's head cracked against the hardwood. The gun flew from his hands.

The masked attacker's weight pressed down against him. The intruder swung. Jackson blocked the punch with his left hand and leveled a hard blow with his right. He caught the man in his jaw. The intruder grunted and fell back.

He leapt to his feet. So did Jackson.

"RCMP!" Jackson shouted. "You're under arrest for breaking and entering! Hands where I can see them! Now!"

The intruder didn't even hesitate. He leapt over the couch, stepped across the table and ran for the open back door. The man dashed out into the night. Jackson scrambled for his gun, reholstered it and ran after him.

As he got outside, he caught a glimpse of the attacker disappearing through the trees, following the same path Jackson had found before. The criminal was moving so stealthily that Jackson couldn't even hear him. But he knew where the man was going.

Jackson pushed himself faster, praying with every step. Then the trees parted. The dark waters lay ahead. The masked man was standing up in a small speedboat, using an oar to push far enough away from the shore that he could hit the engine without wrecking the propeller on the ground.

Jackson planted his feet in the earth and raised his weapon, silently praying to God that he wouldn't have to take the shot.

"Stop!" Jackson shouted. "I'm—"

"I know who you are, Officer Locke!" the man shouted. His accent was thick and sounded Irish. "And if you fire that gun, you'll never find out what happened to your sister!"

Gemma?

"Where is she?" Jackson shouted. "What happened to her?"

What looked like a long grenade glinted in the man's hand. He yanked the pin.

Suddenly, a blinding light overwhelmed Jackson's eyes and a deafening bang sounded in the air. Smoke filled Jackson's senses. He heard the boat motor roar and when his eyesight cleared, the intruder was gone.

FIVE

Amy sat bolt upright as a boom echoed through the air.

Was it gunfire? An explosion?

Please, Lord, let Jackson be okay.

With one hand, Amy cradled Skye in her belly. With the other she reached down for Hudson's comforting bulk. She could feel the rumble of the dog's soft growl reverberating through her fingertips.

Somehow she'd actually managed to doze off in the bunk while praying. She'd felt strangely comfortable and at peace alone in the camper, for reasons she couldn't begin to understand, only then to be jolted awake by what sounded like a hundred bullets being fired at once.

Her ears scanned the darkness. But silence had fallen outside again, leaving her with no clue about what had just happened. Had Jackson managed to stop the intruder? Or had the criminal gotten the better of him?

Then Hudson's ears perked. The dog's tail began to wag happily, banging like a drumbeat against the camper floor.

Moments later she heard a gentle knock.

"Amy?" Jackson whispered. "It's me. Jackson. It's okay. He's gone."

Thank You, Lord.

Amy slipped her feet over the edge of the cot, feeling the warmth of Hudson's fur brush against her legs. Amy's fingers fumbled as she unlocked the door and pushed it open. There stood Jackson, looking tired and breathing heavily. She guessed he'd run back through the woods.

"Sorry to take the extra second getting back to you," he said, "but I stopped for these."

He held up her running shoes.

"You stopped to get my shoes?" she asked.

"Well, yeah." He grinned almost sheepishly. "I thought you'd want them. Right? I mean, unless you want me to keep carrying you around everywhere."

A grateful sob slipped past her lips, as if her brain had finally caught up with her overwhelming sense of relief at seeing him standing there. Suddenly she found herself throwing her arms around him. He wrapped his free arm around her and brushed his hand along her back.

"Hey, hey," Jackson said, softly. "I'm okay. He's gone. You're safe. I'm safe. It's all good."

Just as quickly as she'd grabbed onto him, she let go again. Why had she hugged him like that?

"Are you okay?" Jackson asked.

"Yeah," she said. Amy stepped back, then took her shoes from his hand and dropped them on the floor. She wriggled her feet into them, oddly thankful for the distraction.

"Do you want a hand with that?" Jackson asked.

"No, I've had a lot of practice in recent weeks," Amy said. He waited until she'd successfully gotten her shoes on, then reached for her hand to help her out of the camper. She took his hand, feeling the warmth of his fingers on hers. Amy's arms still seemed to tingle from the spontaneous hug they'd shared just moments ago. She pulled her hand out of his. "Thank you."

Hudson jumped down from the camper. Jackson closed the door and they started walking back to the cottage.

"So, what happened?" she asked. "I heard a really loud bang. It sounded like something exploded."

Jackson broke her gaze.

"Unfortunately, he got away," Jackson said. "He was in the cabin, we tussled, he ran out through the woods and hopped in a boat. And I lost him. He had a flash bang."

She looked up. "What's that?"

They kept walking, with Hudson flanking Jackson on his other side. Jackson still wouldn't meet her eye.

"It's sometimes called either a stun grenade or flash grenade," he said. "You pull the pin, there's a big bang, a really bright flash of light and sometimes a bit of smoke. They're used by the military and law enforcement for crowd control and to disorient hostiles."

"You're making him sound like a magician," she said. "Big flash of light, puff of smoke and ta-da he's gone."

She was trying to lighten the mood, and Jackson almost smiled at that. But he seemed too frustrated with himself to be shaken by the joke.

"All we've got here is a canoe," Amy said. "But the neighboring cottage has left us the keys to their motorboat. The keys are in the kitchen."

"Thanks, but I don't think I'm going to find any trace of him now," Jackson said. There was an odd tone to his voice she'd never heard before. It was bitter and frustrated, maybe even embarrassed. "Whoever this guy is, I think we're dealing with a professional. The question is, a professional what? You were not kidding when you said he moved silently. But his fighting skills were more opportunistic than calculated."

"So, a professional thief?" she asked. "Or a professional hit man?"

"I can't know for sure," he said. "But I'd definitely say he's skilled at breaking and entering."

"Plus, he came prepared." Instinctively, Amy ran her hand over her neck, remembering the cloth bag he'd yanked over her head just a few hours earlier.

Jackson shook his head. "He was running through the woods and I couldn't even hear him. Plus, he was methodical. The cottage barely looked touched."

Still, his eyes were looking everywhere except her face. Uneasiness grew in the pit of her stomach. There was something else bothering him. Something else was troubling his mind, but he wouldn't say it.

She stopped and turned to him.

"What aren't you telling me?" she asked.

Jackson stopped and blew out a long breath.

"I chased him down to the waterfront," he said. He started walking again and so did she. "When I got there, he was pushing a small speedboat out into the water. It's so shallow there that he had to get out a ways before he dropped the motor so that he wouldn't destroy it on the rocks. I identified myself as a police officer. I also pulled my weapon, which was a dicey move, because honestly it would've been a pretty tricky shot from that distance, especially in the darkness."

"And?" Amy pressed.

"And he shouted that if I fired that gun, I'd never find out what happened to Gemma."

Amy's whole body jolted as if her heart had suddenly stopped. She stumbled forward a step and felt Jackson's hand quickly take her arm and hold her up.

"You okay?" he asked.

"I'm fine." Amy shook him off. "You're saying the man who attacked me in the bookstore and who broke into the cottage knows where Gemma is and what happened to her? Does that mean he kidnapped her? Did he kill her?"

"I don't know," Jackson said, "and we can't jump to conclusions."

Maybe not. But that still didn't explain the odd shift in Jackson's tone. Something had happened between the time he'd dropped her off in the camper and returned. Whatever it was had shaken him.

"He did have a heavy accent like you said," Jackson added. "But it sounded more Irish to me. Either way, I think it's probably fake. Thankfully, I have two colleagues coming up tomorrow to provide extra hands on this case. Constable Caleb Perry, who you talked to on the phone, and also Constable Blake Murphy. Sorry, I confirmed it after you'd gone to bed for the night and forgot to mention it earlier in all the excitement."

They got to the cottage. Jackson stretched his

hand over the doorknob. Then he hesitated. "I think I should stay in the living room for the rest of the night. If that's okay with you. I don't want to run the risk of that guy coming back. Hudson can stay on the porch."

"Hudson can camp out in the living room with you," Amy said quickly. She ran her hand over the back of the K-9's neck. "We made peace back in the camper. Hudson and I are good now."

And for some reason, right now, I might actually trust him more than you. At least I know he's not hiding anything from me.

Jackson nodded. "Sounds good."

He opened the door and switched on the light. Finally, she could see the full contours of his face. It was still a little puffy, but his skin had mostly recovered from the bear spray. Dark shadows lined his eyes. He looked tired and worried, like he'd aged a decade since they'd said good-night.

"Hudson and I are just going to do a quick check of the place to make sure all the doors and windows are locked, so we don't have any unwanted visitors," he said. "We'll be back in a second."

He signaled Hudson to his side and turned as if he was about to head to the second floor.

Amy grabbed his arm. He looked back.

"I'm choosing to trust you," she said. "I believe you're a good guy and if you're keeping something from me it has to be for a good reason. But I can tell you're hiding something. There's something else on your mind—something you're not telling me. My ex told me enough lies to last a lifetime and I can't take any more now. So please, tell me what happened, Jackson. Why do you seem so shaken?"

He knew I was Gemma's brother, Jackson thought as he searched Amy's deep and earnest gaze. *Which means, somehow, he knows more about this whole situation than I do. And he knows more about me than you. What does that even mean?*

Jackson wished he could open up and talk to Amy about it. About all of it. But unfortunately, he'd made a rash and foolish decision the day before that had put him in a stupid situation. And now the last thing he wanted to do was upset Amy any more than she already was. What if she kicked him out of the cottage in the middle of the night and the masked intruder came back? What if she got attacked again and hurt—or worse— because of his mistake?

He could forgive himself—mostly—for the rash decision in the moment. But that call was getting harder to defend with every passing hour. It was like he'd drunk something corrosive, mistakenly believing it would be the best medicine, and ever since he felt it eating away his insides.

Amy was still standing in front of him, looking at him expectantly.

"The masked man told me that he knew who I was," Jackson said, dancing as close to the truth as he could. "That really rattled me. Maybe that means he knows I've been looking into the case. Or maybe he somehow saw my badge. I don't know. But I didn't want to worry you. Because, for all I know, he was lying to me and doesn't have any idea where Gemma is."

"But he knows about her," Amy said. "He knows she's missing and you're looking for her."

Jackson nodded.

"But he didn't say anything specific about where she was, what happened to her or even if she's still alive?" Amy pressed.

"No," Jackson said.

Still, she searched his face for a long moment as if trying to decipher a deeper truth hidden behind his eyes. He'd tell her that he was Gemma's brother tomorrow when Caleb and Blake were there for backup. Then it wouldn't matter if she hated him, because at least she'd be safe.

He was the one who'd drunk the poison. He could live with it eating him up inside until then.

Amy waited in the living room while Jackson and Hudson did a thorough check of the cottage.

But aside from a few drawers he could tell had been opened and books he could tell had been moved, nothing was amiss.

When he got back to the living room, he found Amy had laid out a mountain of blankets and pillows on one end of the couch for him, and another blanket on the floor in front of the couch for Hudson. The dog promptly walked over to his new bed and curled up into a ball.

Amy was in the kitchen, eating crackers with peanut butter and boiling water.

"I'm making peppermint tea," she said. "If you'd like some. There's some of Gemma's regular tea in the cupboard too. I just haven't been able to handle caffeine since getting pregnant."

"Have you got any instant coffee?" he asked.

She glanced in the cupboard. "Yeah, we've got some of that too." She pulled out an orange container and shook it. "It sounds pretty dry and granular."

"Good by me," he said. "If you can dump about an inch into a mug, and add some hot water and a spoon, I'll take it from there."

A smile crossed her face, and there was something about it that seemed to light up the furthest corners of his exhausted core. "Deal."

He rekindled the fire in the wood-burning stove while Amy put the crackers away and made them hot drinks. A few moments later, they sat in comfortable silence in the living room, in the same chairs they'd been in that evening. Amy and Jackson sipped their respective drinks and glanced at each other over the tops of their mugs. Neither of them seemed to be in any hurry to try to head back to bed and turn in for the night.

"How are your eyes feeling?" she asked.

"Still a bit dry and sore," he said. "But they've mostly recovered."

"Sorry again about that," she said.

"It's really no big deal—"

"Yeah, it is," Amy cut him off. "At least it is to me. I really appreciate the fact you're being so awesome about it."

"But you were totally justified in spraying me in the face like that," Jackson said. "You were startled and defending yourself."

"I don't know how to explain what I mean." She ran a hand through her hair. "But the fact you're right doesn't stop people from yelling at you. I was a waitress and customers yelled at me all the time for things that weren't even a little bit my fault. Not a lot of people are as understanding as you are or as willing to let things just roll off their backs."

Her earnest hazel eyes met his. He held her gaze, and for a long moment neither of them said anything.

"Well, I made a lot of mistakes when I was

younger," he said, finally. "And I know what it's like to want to be forgiven. So, I try not to give anyone a hard time when they mess up. Again, not that I think you did anything wrong."

But he couldn't let himself go down that train of thought. She didn't know that he was Gemma's brother or that she'd once rejected his apology.

"You mentioned that some people have a temper," he said, changing the subject to a safer one. "And as much as I hate to ask you this, I need to find out more about Paul. Did your ex have a bad temper?"

"I think so," Amy said. "Not that I ever saw him yell, but he was pretty particular about having things the way he wanted. I never saw him do anything violent, though."

"Is there any way he could be behind what's happened to Gemma?"

"Well, he's not the intruder," Amy said.

"How can you be sure?"

She sighed. "Look, I know the previous police accused me of not being totally honest, but I have nothing to hide. Just stuff I'm embarrassed by and don't like talking about." Amy rolled her eyes. "To start with, our intruder is about a foot taller than Paul. Also, Paul was a liar and a cheat, but he's not that athletic. Which is ironic, because he always claimed he came from a long line of men who'd served in the military. He loved showing off his grandfather's Second World War medals. They were really impressive ones with wings and crowns and everything."

"Okay," Jackson said. "But what if he hired someone to get revenge on you? Or revenge on Gemma for taking you in? It's not unheard of for a man to leave his wife and then turn around and try to punish her for moving on with her life."

Amy set her mug down on the coffee table with a thump.

"First off, I'll concede that Gemma did spend a lot of time trying to dig into Paul's identity and his various shenanigans after I moved up here," Amy said. "She had this investigative drive, like she'd missed her calling to be a detective or something. She's always been into unsolved mysteries and cold cases. All the dog-eared fiction books in this place are Ajay's and all the true crime ones are hers."

Very true. He'd often thought it was a shame Gemma hadn't gotten into law enforcement. She had an incredibly acute mind. But she'd also always been too independent to even consider it. Not to mention, Gemma felt the police had been too hard on him when he'd been younger—plus they'd botched it when a friend of hers had vanished in college.

"Then we got an email from someone claiming to be Paul's team of powerful lawyers," Amy continued.

"Really?" Jackson leaned forward. "What did it say?"

"It said that Paul wasn't the father of my child," Amy said, "that he wanted nothing to do with me and that he was taking a restraining order out against both me and Gemma."

"Wow." Jackson blew out a hard breath. "What a jerk."

Among other worse terms he resisted the urge to use.

"Yeah," Amy said. "Gemma suspected he'd written the letter himself and pretended to be his own lawyers. Which might be true, but it gave me the closure I needed. I got an annulment, and I asked Gemma to stop looking into Paul because it wasn't good for my stress level. I didn't need to know anything more, and I already felt terrible enough for ever getting involved with him."

Okay, but that didn't mean Gemma had actually stopped digging.

"I'm glad she looked into Paul for a while," Amy went on. "There's a lot of stuff that I only know about because of her."

"Like what?" Jackson pressed.

"He told me his name was Paul Keebles," Amy said. "He told me that he was incredibly wealthy, worked in real estate and lived in California. He said he was never married, no kids, and that his grandfather was a military veteran. Also, he claimed he visited Niagara Falls at least once a month on business."

"What kind of business?" Jackson asked.

"He said he had an important business contact up here," Amy said, "and they were doing some real estate deals. But I never met him and for all I know he had other women he was visiting in Niagara Falls."

She spread her hands as if laying out the information she had.

"Gemma found out that he doesn't work in real estate or live in California," Amy said. "He has two other wives in different states, at least one fiancée and multiple children. He goes by several different names, including Paul Brown, Paul Keane, Paul Kent and Stanley Paul. His only career seems to be catfishing women, stealing small amounts of money and valuables from them, and moving on. Gross low-level stuff."

Jackson could feel heat building at the back of his neck. He took a calming breath.

How can anyone treat people that way?

"Did you try contacting these other women and warning them?" he asked, gently.

"Gemma did, and I think that's partly what sparked that letter from his lawyers."

She ran the back of her hand over her eyes, as if trying to wipe away unseen tears.

"Paul doesn't care about me!" Her voice rose

and quivered with what sounded like anger. "He doesn't care about anyone. He discards people. He dumps wives, leaves children and moves on. I wasn't special to him. All I ever was to him was a little blip in a long string of cons."

Jackson winced. There was a pain in his chest that felt so sharp it was like he'd been shot.

"So, I really don't think he'd hire some Australian slash Irish professional thief to go after me now," Amy added. "Because I'm no threat to him and there's nothing I have that he wants. But if you think it'll help in the investigation, I'm happy to tell the whole messy story about me and Paul." She pulled her long honey brown hair back into a ponytail and tied it with an elastic that she'd produced from somewhere he didn't see. "Well, maybe 'happy' is the wrong word. But I'm willing to tell you everything that happened, if you think it'll help."

"At the very least it will help me eliminate him as a suspect," Jackson said.

He set his mug down and leaned forward, with his elbows on his knees, as Amy told the story about how Paul had wooed her, tricked her into spontaneously eloping with him, then robbed her and abandoned her. Her voice was matter-of-fact, and more angry than sad. But as she talked, the pain in his core continued to grow until it felt like his entire body ached for her and what she'd gone through.

"When I first realized he'd left, my immediate instinct was to just try calling him over and over again," Amy said. "Which is ridiculous considering my number had been blocked, my bank account had been drained and every valuable gift he'd ever given me was gone. I was a total mess when Gemma came to get me. I don't know where I'd be without her."

Jackson silently thanked God that his sister had been there for Amy.

"Gemma insisted I call the cops," Amy said. "But there wasn't much they could do considering he was an American citizen and most of the stuff he'd taken were gifts he'd given me."

"Which I'm sure didn't do much to help the fact Gemma doesn't trust cops," Jackson said.

Amy glanced at him sharply. "How did you know Gemma doesn't trust cops?"

Right. Because he wasn't Gemma's brother. He was a stranger. But he was so exhausted and caught up in Amy's story, he'd momentarily forgotten his cover.

"You know that a few years ago, one of Gemma's college roommates disappeared near Manitoulin Island?" he asked.

"Yeah." Amy nodded. "Her name was Louise

Roch. She'd been on a boat, and they believed she went overboard, but they never found her body."

"Well, Gemma apparently was really frustrated with how the police handled it," Jackson said. "She tried to contact the press and sent a lot of letters to different law enforcement agencies."

All of that was true, and he hoped she'd believe that any cop who was looking into Gemma's disappearance would've uncovered it.

"For all we know, Gemma's disappearance now could be connected to that cold case," Jackson said. "Not that law enforcement has found any evidence of that."

Amy nodded again. Then she picked up her mug and took another sip, even though he suspected the tea might be cold.

"Well, now you know the whole story about Paul," Amy said. "At least as far as I know it."

He wanted to envelop Amy in his arms. He wanted to hug her like she'd hugged him back at the camper, tell her that he was so sorry someone had treated her that way and that he'd do everything in his power to make sure no one ever hurt her again. Instead, he crossed his arms over his chest, mirroring her posture, and leaned even further back against the sofa, rooted there by the knowledge that he had no right to hug her. She didn't know who he was, she didn't like the guy he'd been when he was younger, and she'd dislike him even more in a few hours when she found out the truth.

"I'm so sorry," he said. "I wish there was something I could do."

She nodded, yawning, then said she was still planning on waking up early and getting to the bookstore to see about getting the power back on.

Jackson stood as she got up, took her mug and offered to tidy up the dishes.

He tracked her with his eyes as she slowly walked up the spiral staircase and down the hallway to the bedroom that had once been his. The door closed and the lock clicked. But still he stood there for a long moment staring at the closed door and wishing he knew what to say to take her pain away. Then finally he let out a long breath and started tidying the kitchen.

Hudson lay asleep on his blanket in front of the couch. But as Jackson approached, Hudson opened his eyes. The dog's eyebrows rose.

"It's okay, buddy," Jackson said. "Get some sleep while you can. I have a feeling that tomorrow is going to be a long day."

The dog closed his eyes and settled his head back down again. Within moments he could hear the gentle wheeze of Hudson snoring. Jackson wished he could fall asleep so easily.

Instead, he found himself stretching out on the couch with blankets draped over his body and his eyes scanning the ceiling beams in the darkness. He drifted in and out of a fitful sleep, praying for answers that didn't come. Finally, the morning sun began to rise over the lake, casting the water below in pink and orange hues.

Soon afterward he heard the sound of Amy's footsteps as she made her way downstairs. He sat up and looked at his watch. It was quarter to seven.

"I hope I didn't wake you," she said. "Skye tends to rise with the sun and start kicking up a storm."

"Not a problem." Jackson swung his legs over the side of the couch.

Hudson leaped to his feet and ran over to greet Amy as soon as she reached the main floor. She smiled and ran her hand over the dog's head. "Good morning, Hudson."

"How did you sleep?" Jackson asked.

"Not too bad, all things considered," she said. She looked up at him. "How about you?"

"About as good as I could expect." He stood. "I should probably go take Hudson for a walk."

"I was planning on making French toast," Amy said. "Good by you?"

He smiled. "Good by me."

Her tone was friendly and polite, and a million miles away from the emotional closeness he'd felt with her the night before. Instinctively, he mirrored her tone and they stood there, smiling nicely at each other. He signaled Hudson to his side. Jackson and his partner walked out the front door across the porch and down toward the lake. The memory of how Amy had thrown her arms around him in a spontaneous hug the night before flickered at the back of his mind.

Had she regretted getting so close? Or being so vulnerable with Jackson when she'd opened up about her ex-husband?

Maybe Amy was intentionally putting distance between them, and if so maybe it was a good thing. It definitely wouldn't hurt for him to do the same.

When Amy found out the truth about him, she'd be understandably upset. And if watching the implosion of his parent's marriage had taught him anything it was that conflict lead to yelling, anger, insults and worse. There was no way he could imagine she'd ever forgive him for what he'd done. The best he could hope for now was to somehow lessen the blow.

He walked slowly down to the water, letting Hudson run on ahead of him. He checked his phone. It was barely seven and the RCMP's Ontario K-9 Unit wouldn't open until nine. He needed to check in with Finnick and fill him in, but he also wasn't about to wake his boss up.

He could however wake up Caleb.

The phone rang four times. Then Caleb's voice was on the line, sounding slightly more alert than Jackson guessed he was. "Hey."

"Good morning," Jackson said.

"Is it really?" Caleb chuckled. "I'll take your word for it."

"Did I wake you up?" Jackson asked.

"Nah," Caleb said. "I was just staring at the coffee maker telling it to hurry up. How's your face?"

"Only slightly more haggard than usual."

"Ha." Caleb snorted.

Jackson quickly filled him in on everything that had happened in the night, including his suspicion that the intruder was a professional.

Caleb whistled. "Well, that woke me up fast. I'm going to meet with Finnick and Blake in the office in a bit. Then I should reach Clearwater around two thirty. Okay?"

"Sounds good," Jackson said. That would give him a few hours to figure out how to tell Amy that he was Gemma's brother and apologize for being an idiot. "We're going to be heading to the bookstore in a little bit. The power was out yesterday and she really wants to get it open and running by nine. I figure it's as good a place to hunker down and wait for you guys as any. And it'll probably be good for Amy's health and sense of well-being to be focused on the store today."

"And Amy still doesn't know that Gemma's your sister, right?" Caleb checked.

"Nope," Jackson said. "But apparently our professional thief does."

"Wow. Okay." Caleb seemed to stretch the two words out into a few dozen syllables.

"By the way, thanks for covering for me when she called yesterday," Jackson said.

"No problem," Caleb said. "I hated doing it, though. I was so impressed she thought to verify your identity."

"Well, Amy's pretty smart." That was an understatement. "I'll see you at the bookstore this afternoon."

"See you then."

Jackson disconnected and called Hudson. Together they headed back into the cottage. Turned out Amy had made enough French toast to feed a small battalion, along with a fresh pot of coffee, which he knew was just for his benefit. She'd also opened one of the cans of dog food he'd set out on the counter the night before and scooped it into Hudson's food bowl. She'd even gotten the dog fresh water.

He let her know that his colleagues should be there after lunch and would meet them at the bookstore. They ate mostly in silence, punctuated by the kind of small talk about the weather that one might make with a stranger when stuck in a slow-moving checkout line. Although Amy smiled frequently and even generously, somehow her eyes never lit up the way they had the night before. When breakfast was done, they did the dishes side by side, with her washing and him drying.

Then the three of them headed to the store, this time taking his truck, with Amy in the passenger seat and Hudson spread out in the back. Finally, they pulled into the narrow alley behind the shop.

She got out of the truck, walked toward the door and paused. She turned back. Worry filled her eyes.

He opened the back door for Hudson. "What's wrong?"

"The door is ajar," she said. "It isn't locked and I'm positive I locked it."

"Get behind me," he said.

He pulled his weapon and signaled Hudson to his side. He crossed the alley, pushed the door open and stepped inside.

His heart sank. The lock had been busted. Shelves had been knocked over. Books covered the floor.

The store had been ransacked.

SIX

"What's wrong?" Amy asked as she watched Jackson's body freeze.

"There's been a break-in," Jackson said. His voice was eerily calm and level, but that didn't stop her heart from plummeting into her gut. "Stay behind me."

She waited just outside the doorway as Jackson and Hudson moved through the shop.

"We're all clear," Jackson called from within, "but I've got to warn you, it's a mess."

She stepped through the doorway. Sorrow crushed her core as she scanned the wreckage of their precious little store. The power was still off but enough light streamed in through the large front windows to reveal that every single book had been knocked off the shelf. The bulletin board and her framed sketches had been torn down from the wall.

"Did Gemma have a bird?" Jackson asked.

"There's an empty cage in the other room, but no bird."

Oh no.

"Reepi!" She called the bird's name but didn't hear his cheerful chirping in response.

Where was Gemma's beloved parrot? Amy slid past him and ran into the side room. Her heart shattered. Reepi's empty cage was lying on the floor. The door was open. Green and gray feathers were scattered around the room.

The bird was gone.

Tears rushed to her eyes and she didn't fully succeed in blinking them back before Jackson saw them.

"Are you okay?" he asked, softly.

His comforting hand brushed her shoulder. Hudson's warm body pressed against her leg.

"Gemma had a conure parrot," she said. "His name was Reepi. He was only a few months old. But she loved him so much. I can't believe I lost him."

Hudson went over and sniffed the cage thoughtfully.

"Hey, it's okay," Jackson said. "He probably flew outside. The door was open a crack when we got here."

She ran her fingers over her eyes. "I don't know why I'm crying. He was only a bird."

"But he was family?" Jackson asked.

Amy nodded. "Yeah. Gemma really adored him and he kept me company after she was gone."

His hand ran along her back. It was comforting and supportive.

"Hudson's like family to me," Jackson said. "If anything ever happened to him, I'd be devastated."

How was it this man she barely knew sometimes seemed to know the exact right thing to say?

Jackson stepped away from her and went over to where Hudson was still poking around the cage. He ran both hands over the dog's head and a thoughtful look crossed his face. Jackson knelt down beside his partner, picked a feather up off the ground and held it up in front of Hudson's nose. The dog sniffed the feather obediently. A tiny ray of hope flickered in her chest.

"Search," Jackson ordered his partner. "Find Reepi."

Hudson's ears perked. The dog barked.

"Show me!" Jackson said.

Hudson woofed again, as if agreeing. The dog turned and trotted out into the main room.

"Is Hudson really able to track Reepi?" Amy asked.

"I don't know," Jackson said. "But he seems to think he can."

Hudson barked sharply as if telling them to

hurry up. They walked through the main room and found him standing by the back door. Jackson and Amy followed the K-9 out of the store, through the narrow alleyway, past Jackson's vehicle, and then out into the thick and untamed woods. Trees hemmed in around them on all sides. The German shepherd confidently cut his own path through the forest.

"Reepi!" she called.

She glanced at Jackson. Deep lines creased his brow.

"Are you okay?" she asked.

"Honestly, I have no idea if this is going to work, and I'm worried about getting your hopes up. I don't want to let you down."

"Thank you for telling me that," she said. Instinctively, she reached for his fingers and squeezed them. "I appreciate your honesty."

She held his hand for a long moment before realizing what she was doing and letting go.

"Hey, Reepi!" Jackson cupped his hands around his mouth. "Little bird buddy! It's time for breakfast!"

He glanced at Amy and whispered, "It *is* time for his breakfast, right?"

"Yeah." She glanced at him gratefully. He met her eyes and smiled.

They reached a small clearing in the woods. The dog stopped suddenly. Amy held her breath and prayed. There was silence at first, and then something rustled in the branches above their heads.

As they watched, the parrot fluttered down from the trees in a magnificent display of gray and green. Amy's hand rose to her lips. The bird landed on the dog's head.

A laugh slipped through her fingers, mingled with a sob.

Jackson exhaled, and she wondered how long he'd been holding his breath.

"Thank You, God," Jackson prayed. Then he glanced down at his partner and ran his hand over his side. "Good job."

Amy reached out her hand for the bird, but Reepi bounced down onto Hudson's back and busied himself with cleaning his feathers.

"Well, he seems happy with his new perch," Jackson said. "Maybe he's tired from his adventures."

He chuckled, she did too, and then they turned and walked back through the woods to the store, with Reepi riding on Hudson.

It wasn't until they were back indoors that Reepi disembarked and flew through the main room back into the smaller side room. Within moments she heard his usual chirping as he bounced around the bookshelves. Jackson ran his hand silently over his partner's head and scratched him behind the ears. Amy followed the sound of the chirping bird into the other room.

For a moment, she'd been so elated about finding Reepi that she'd almost forgotten just how terrible a mess the place was. So many books were scattered on the floor there was barely anywhere to stand. She turned a small round table that had displayed large artistic picture books right side up again, and started stacking books on it.

Suddenly the lights flickered on above and she could hear the beep of the store's Wi-Fi router coming online.

"Eureka!" Jackson called. A moment later he appeared through the door. "Turns out our intruder cut a few electrical wires. Thankfully I'm handy enough with a pocketknife to splice them back together. Although, you're going to want to get an actual electrician in to do the job right."

"I'm guessing he wished he'd left the power on before he realized he'd have to come back to ransack the store," Amy said, wryly. "But my guess is our criminal hasn't been doing a lot of planning. He attacked me, thinking he'd get what he was after. When that didn't work, he tried searching the cottage. Then when that failed, he came back here."

"It's a good theory." Jackson looked around at the books on the floor. "How can I help?"

Something about the simple question warmed

her heart. Cleaning up the store wasn't his responsibility. But he had her back without a second thought.

"Fiction goes on the right wall, alphabetically by author," she said. "Left wall is nonfiction and the back wall is for crime, cold cases and unsolved mysteries. There are a lot of those. Gemma loves them. I'll sort the children's and coffee-table books."

"Got it," Jackson said.

He started picking his way around the mess. For a long moment, she just stood there and watched him. She'd never met a man like him before. So strong and yet so kind and caring at the same time. She hadn't even realized she was staring until he stopped and looked up at her.

"What?" he asked. He straightened up and ran his hands down his legs.

Heat rose to her cheeks.

"I'm just really thankful that you're here," she admitted. "I know you told me you've made a lot of mistakes in the past and that you don't think you're cut out for family life. But from what I can see, you're a really amazing guy. I hope you're not being too hard on yourself."

She wasn't even sure why she was talking to him about this. But there was something incredible about him—something that drew her in and made her feel safe—and after everything he'd done for her, she hated the thought that he didn't see that in himself.

He swallowed hard.

"Thank you," he said. "But you wouldn't say that if you knew the real me. My parents' marriage was really toxic. And I was a terrible kid. I got into all kinds of trouble. I hate the idea of bringing a child into the world only for him or her to end up like me."

She reached her hand toward him. Her fingers brushed his arm.

"But you've grown since then, right?" she asked. "I don't know what you were like before, but the Jackson I know is helpful, funny, forgiving and kind. Maybe if you had a child, they'd turn out like the person you are now."

Something wavered in his eyes, like he was standing on the edge of a diving board afraid to jump. His mouth opened, and she thought he was about to say something important. Then he closed it again, stepped away and broke her gaze.

"Thank you," he said, after a long moment. He turned his attention back to the mess on the floor. "If your kid turns out anything like her mom, I'm sure she'll be pretty awesome too."

He scooped up a handful of books, turned his back to her and started arranging them onto the shelves. Why was he so uncomfortable receiving compliments?

Lord, whatever is hurting Jackson, and whatever lurks in his past, please help him see himself through Your eyes.

She went back to tidying the books and for a long while neither of them said anything.

"Our silent intruder was really careful when he searched the cottage," Jackson said, eventually. "But he was either angry, frustrated or in a hurry when he ransacked this place. I've never seen a place so thoroughly tossed."

"Maybe he's only quiet and methodical when he's afraid of being caught," Amy suggested. "I'm sure just throwing everything on the floor is a more efficient method of finding what you're after."

"Or maybe he's just really frustrated that this job has taken so long and has started to become more ruthless," Jackson suggested.

She bent down, picked up one of the brand-new picture books and looked at it. She ran her finger down the crisp, clean spine. A thought crossed her mind. "Remember I mentioned I wanted to search every book in this place for hidden messages? The state he left the store in practically confirms that he was looking for the laptop or at least something around that size."

Jackson's eyebrows rose. "How do you figure?"

"Well, he was clearly looking for something small enough to fit in a drawer but too big to fit in a book." Amy bent down and picked up two more coffee-table books. "He didn't flip the pages or look through these. Their spines are still pristine."

"Good point," Jackson said. "None of the children's books look leafed through either." He glanced back into the other room. "Also, he didn't open any of the VHS video or DVD cases. We can't assume it was a search for the laptop that caused all this chaos, but it's the likely culprit."

Reepi chirped loudly from somewhere above their heads, as if announcing that he knew the answer.

Jackson chuckled. "Why couldn't Gemma have gotten one of those talking parrots that solve crimes in adventure novels? It would be kind of nice if Reepi could just solve the crime for us."

She laughed. "Well, conures can be taught some words," Amy said. "But he's still pretty young."

Jackson looked up. "Where'd he go anyway? I can hear him, but I can't see him."

"Gemma just lets him fly around free range when the store's not busy," Amy said. "His favorite spot is the back wall. He likes to hide behind the books on the top shelf."

"Well, there are no books there now." Jackson stood on his tiptoes and looked up. "And I don't see him up there."

"Huh, well, I can definitely hear him."

Amy nudged a stool over to the back wall with her foot and stepped up on it.

"Be careful," Jackson said. "Let me steady you."

She felt his hand against the small of her back. "Thank you."

"Do you see him?"

"No," she said. She scanned the empty shelf, her confusion growing. "It's like he's vanished."

But she could hear the bird chirping as loudly and cheerfully as ever. Then she saw it, a dark gap in the wood on the back of the top shelf. "I think I've found a hole, though."

"A hole?" Jackson repeated. "Do you think we have a mouse?"

"I hope not. Hang on, I'm going to check it out." She walked her hands along the wood, then ran her fingers around it. "It's definitely a hole. It's perfectly round and smooth."

"How big?" Jackson asked.

"Maybe three inches?"

She slid her fingers into the hole and felt something move underneath her touch. There was a click. Then suddenly the entire wall of shelves gave way in front of her.

Jackson's jaw dropped as a huge section of the back wall swung open in front of them. Amy pitched forward as she lost her grip on the shelf. Quickly, Jackson wrapped his arms around her, just below her baby bump, and pulled her back against his chest. Darkness filled the space in front of him where the wall of books had been. Reepi shot through the opening in the doorway and soared over their heads.

Jackson felt the gentle flutter of Amy's unborn baby against his palm, as if Skye was wondering who the unfamiliar hand belonged to.

"Are you okay?" he asked.

"Yeah," Amy said. "I just wasn't expecting that to happen."

"Neither was I," he said.

He held her steady as she stepped onto the floor.

"Thank you," Amy said. She stepped away from him and through the doorway that had opened in the wall.

"Be careful," he said.

She seemed to be feeling around for a light switch. An instant later a light flickered on with a gentle white glow.

"Wow." Amy exhaled and rocked back on her heels.

He followed her into the room and instantly saw what had taken her breath away.

A giant map of the country covered the wall, surrounded by dozens and dozens of newspaper clippings, sticky notes and computer printouts, many of which were connected to the map by thumbtacks and pieces of string.

"Well, I guess this answers the question of whether or not Gemma was hiding a secret," he said.

"Do you think this is what the intruder was looking for?" Amy said.

"Well, it's bigger than a book," Jackson said, "but doesn't explain why he was opening drawers or checking the cottage. I'm guessing this is where Gemma hid whatever it is he's looking for."

He took a step back and looked around, while Amy studied the wall. The room itself was long and narrow, about five feet deep, and stretched across the entire length of the adjacent room. He guessed it had once been intended as a storage room before Gemma had converted it into some kind of secret office. A small antique desk completely filled the space at the end of the room to his right. It was covered in even more papers, maps, and books on both law and criminology. A power bar lay on the floor with both laptop and phone cables plugged into it.

"We've got chargers but no laptop," Jackson said. "So, if I'm right in my guess that he was looking for Gemma's laptop, this might've been where she kept it."

Amy continued to scan the wall.

"These are all old crime stories," she said. "They're murders mostly, but also a few thefts and some missing people." She stepped back. "Some of them are ten, twenty, even fifty years old."

"They're all cold cases," Jackson said. Although he still had no idea why his sister had built herself a secret room dedicated to investigating them. "My boss, Inspector Finnick, is really interested in cases like these. He might be able to shed some light on all this."

"Finnick." Amy turned and her eyebrows rose. "Your boss has the same last name as you? Are you two related?"

Heat rose to the back of Jackson's neck. He broke her gaze. "No relation."

Finnick had warned him the night before that he was foolish to just wing his cover. And maybe he should've really sat down and done the work to develop a more solid backstory. Then again, he hadn't expected he'd need to. He'd been planning to hold her at arm's length. Instead, it seemed like with every conversation they somehow kept growing closer.

Amy didn't say anything for a long moment. When he glanced back, she had the same sharp look in her eyes that she'd had last night when he'd mentioned Gemma didn't like cops.

Help me, Lord. I made a big mistake yesterday and I don't know how to fix it.

He could feel something inside him prompting him to tell her the truth, immediately, without hesitation or even pausing to come up with the right words.

But he couldn't. Not yet. Not until backup arrived and he knew Amy was safe. Until then, he needed to make sure she trusted him to protect her.

She looked past him at the papers on the table.

"Hang on." She walked over. "It looks like Gemma was trying to get her private investigator's license."

"What?" Jackson turned. His sister was training to be a private detective?

"Look." Amy spread papers out across the desk. "These are all modules from the official Ontario Private Investigator Study Guide. This here is a practice copy of the test. She wasn't just interested in solving crime. She was actually going for it."

He sucked in a breath like he'd just been punched in the gut. His big sister was studying how to solve crime and had never breathed a word to him about it. Why? Didn't she trust him? He had chosen a career in official law enforcement, and here his own sister thought so little of cops like him that she'd decided to be a civilian detective...

He stopped and repented of the petty thought the moment he caught it crossing his mind. Maybe she'd tried to talk to him and he hadn't listened. Or maybe they'd sniped at each other so many times in the past, she hadn't even tried.

Lord, how did my relationship with my sister get so broken?

"I had no idea about any of this." Amy shook her head. "I can't believe she felt she had to hide something this important from me."

"I'm sure she was just trying to protect you," Jackson said. "She knew you were stressed and dealing with a lot. Maybe she just didn't want to worry you about this, especially if she wasn't even sure when she was going to take the test."

"She used to talk about wanting a career change or going back to school," Amy said. "But for the past year she's just been spending all her time at the bookstore. I had no idea this was the reason why. I don't understand."

Jackson reached out a hand to comfort her. But instead he stopped himself, pulled back and crossed his arms.

"I don't know either," he admitted. "But I'm pretty sure the last thing Gemma wanted to do was upset you, and she wouldn't want you to blame yourself now." He turned back to the wall. "But this puts Gemma's disappearance in a whole new light, doesn't it?"

"You think somebody connected to one of these cases has something to do with what happened to her?" Amy asked.

"Unfortunately, yeah," Jackson said. Here he'd suspected Gemma had kept looking into the petty conman who'd ruined Amy's life. But the array of murders, criminals and downright evil on display on the wall in front of him totally eclipsed all that.

What if his sister had gone after a cold-blooded killer who didn't want to be found?

He closed his eyes and prayed for her safety as his heart ached with the diminishing hope that his sister was still alive.

"I think I know where she was going when she disappeared!" Amy grabbed his arm as her voice suddenly cut through his fear.

He opened his eyes as she pointed at something on Gemma's desk.

"Look, this whole file is about these three mysterious deaths that happened at Pine Crest Retirement Home twelve years ago," she said. Hope shone in her eyes. "There was this string of thefts. People complained they were missing jewelry, money and war memorabilia. Then three different seniors died within a month of each other."

Jackson looked down at the pages. He felt Hudson's head buffet against the back of his knee. Jackson reached back to stroke the dog's head.

Three murders at a seniors' home that happened over a decade ago? How could that have anything to do with his sister's disappearance?

"Look." Amy laid a printed map in the center of the desk and pointed. "Pine Crest Retirement Home is less than a ten-minute drive from the place where Gemma's car was found. What if she found a lead? What if the killer discovered that Gemma was on his tail...and took her out before she could catch him?"

Half an hour later, they were back at the cottage. Jackson could tell that as much as Amy wanted to open the store, both the scale of the cleanup job required and the discovery of the hidden room and Gemma's secret investigations had thrown her for too much of a loop. He'd taken pictures of every inch of the office and sent them to Finnick. He'd picked up everything he could find on the Pine Crest case, while Amy had coaxed Reepi back into his cage. Then Jackson had driven Amy, Reepi, Hudson and himself back to the cottage.

Now he sat on the couch and flipped through the Pine Crest file while he waited for Finnick to call him back. Reepi chirped happily in his cage from his new home on the dining room shelf.

Hudson lay on the floor in front of the cage and watched his new friend bounce back and forth. Amy stood at the kitchen counter, eating crackers dipped in peanut butter and sketching something in a large pad.

Jackson spread the details of the case out on the coffee table. Twelve years ago, a retirement home near South River, Ontario, had experienced a series of petty thefts. At first, people had questioned whether items were just being misplaced, but as time went on it became pretty clear they had a thief on their hands. Then, within a few days of each other, three of the residents passed away—Mitsy Therwell, Angela Jeffries and Gordon Donnelly. All three deaths had seemed to be of natural causes at first, until the coroner found elevated amounts of painkillers in their systems. It seemed that someone had tampered with the doses on their IVs, maybe for no other reason than to put them to sleep so that someone could pilfer their belongings. All three families reported their loved ones had things stolen from them. Initially, suspicion had fallen on a maintenance man named Kenny Stanton. But police had cleared him and then hadn't been able to locate him when they wanted to do a follow-up interview.

Fresh hope fluttered in Jackson's chest. For the first time since he'd learned of his sister's disappearance, he had an actual idea of what she'd been up to and where she might've been going the day she vanished. This could be it. Somewhere in the pages laid out in front of him could be the answer to where his sister was and how to bring her home.

Jackson's phone began to ring. He glanced at the screen.

Finnick.

He looked from where Amy stood by the counter to where his partner lay.

"Just give me a second," he said. "I'm going to take this."

Hudson's ears twitched in Jackson's direction. Amy glanced up, smiled and went back to her sketching.

Jackson stepped out the sliding door onto the back porch and closed it behind him.

"Finnick!" he said. "I'm guessing you've seen the photos. What a surprise, eh? I guess we now know what Gemma's big secret was."

"Hi, Jackson," Finnick said, and something in his tone made the fledgling hope that Jackson had begun to feel start sinking like a lead balloon. "I've seen the pictures and we can talk about them in a moment, but first I'm afraid I have some bad news."

Jackson glanced behind him and double-checked Amy wasn't close enough to listen in.

Then he leaned his elbows against the railing and looked out at the water.

"Hit me," he said.

"I'm sorry to inform you that Ontario Provincial Police think they've found your sister's body," Finnick said. "I'm sorry, but it seems Gemma might be gone."

SEVEN

It was like someone had punched their fist straight into Jackson's rib cage, grabbed ahold of his heart and crushed it. His legs went weak and he almost fell into the railing.

"There's not a lot I can tell you at this point," Finnick went on. His tone was direct but kind. "The body of a Jane Doe was found overnight in the water, downriver from where your sister's car crashed. She had no identification or personal items on her, and her body was badly decomposed. They're running DNA tests now. It'll be a few hours until we know anything for certain, and I can't authorize you to tell Amy Scout until we have more information. Again, I am so sorry."

The door slid open behind him.

"Jackson?" Amy called. "Is everything all right? Is there anything I can do to help?"

He turned. She was standing in the doorway, her face awash with worry and her sketch pad clutched to her chest. He hadn't even realized she'd been watching him. He had no idea what his physical reaction to the news of his sister's potential death had looked like to an outside observer. But now here she was, just steps behind him, checking that he was okay and offering to be there for him.

A lump formed in his throat. He swallowed hard.

"One second," Jackson told Finnick. "I'll call you back."

He ended the call before Finnick responded.

Don't tell her the truth, not until you've got all the information. First get the facts, figure out what you're allowed to tell Amy and how you're going to break it to her, then sit her down and tell her the news.

And yet, at the same time he could hear a second voice, calling out from somewhere deep inside his heart, urging him to tell her everything. He wanted to confess that he was the boy she'd known as Ajay and beg her to forgive him. He wanted to pour out his fear that the body that had been found was Gemma's.

He wanted to pull Amy into his arms, hold her close and promise he'd never be anything but a hundred percent honest with her from now on. But if he did, would she ever be able to forgive him? And even if somehow she did, how could he let himself get close to her knowing that she deserved so much more than a man like him in her life?

"Yeah, I'm okay," Jackson said, hoping his voice sounded more convincing than he felt. "My boss was just warning me some big stuff has come in about a case I'm working on and it caught me off guard. I'm going to go for a walk and call him back." He watched as Amy's lips parted, and he was pretty sure he knew exactly what she was going to ask, so he quickly raised his hand. "If it's about Gemma, I'll fill you in when I can. But I can't tell you anything until I've talked to him. Okay?"

"Okay." Amy nodded.

He looked past her and watched as Hudson got to his feet and started toward him.

"What were you sketching?" Jackson gestured to the pad.

"Us," Amy said. Her face perked up slightly. "Well, me, Gemma and her brother. When we were kids."

She turned the notepad around. There in quick and precise pencil lines were Amy's and Gemma's smiling faces, back when they must've been around thirteen. And behind them, in shadow, he could see himself—Ajay—the boy he'd been and wished he could forget.

But the lines of his face were indistinct and vague, without clear features or form, like he was blending into the shadows around him. Was that how she'd remembered him? Out of focus and lurking in the darkness?

She turned the paper back around.

"I don't know," she said. "I feel like I'm missing something and sketching always helps. I think I'll go sit on the water for a bit while you make your call."

Amy shifted her sketch pad under her arm and pulled her hair back into a ponytail.

"You're going to go sit on the dock?" Jackson asked.

"No," Amy said. "We've got a canoe and I've made an anchor for it. I'm going to push out from shore a bit, anchor myself and sketch."

"You said the neighbors have a motorboat we can borrow," Jackson said. "Why don't you wait until I'm done my call and I'll take you out on the water? I don't like the idea of you going out alone on the lake right now."

"Thanks, but I do this every single day," Amy said. "I have for months. I really like the peace and quiet. Skye enjoys the gentle rocking of the water. And I think I need some time alone to think."

She darted back into the cottage and grabbed a set of pencil crayons. Then she held the door open long enough for Hudson to step through.

The German shepherd looked up at Jackson with big, mournful eyes.

Jackson could tell that Hudson knew he was in pain.

"Don't worry," Amy said. "I'm just going to be floating peacefully in the canoe. I promise I'm not going to drift away. You'll have your eyes on me the entire time, Sergeant."

She pointed to her eyes with two fingers and pointed those fingers at him, as if to lightheartedly emphasize her point. Actually, it wasn't a bad idea. As long as Amy was out on the lake, she wouldn't be able to overhear his conversation with Finnick, and yet she wouldn't be out of view either like she would've been if he'd gone for a walk.

"Yeah, okay," he said. "Just stay where I can see you."

"Will do," she said. Then Amy hesitated. "But are you sure you're fine? You look a little sick."

Her lower lip quivered in apparent worry, even though he could tell by the way she pressed her lips together that she was trying to hide it. Could she tell that he was keeping something from her? Or was she just reeling from the knowledge that Gemma had been keeping such a big secret?

He wanted to pull her close and wrap his arms around her. He wanted to apologize for not admitting he was Gemma's brother sooner and tell her his heart was now breaking over the fact police believed they'd found her dead. Instead, he gave her what he hoped looked like a reassuring smile. "Have fun on the lake."

Amy turned and walked down to the water. She crossed the dock, slid on an oversize life jacket, got in the canoe and undid the rope. She picked up a paddle and pushed off into the water. Jackson's eyes never left her for a second. With slow and lazy strokes Amy paddled out until she was about two thirds of the way between the shore and the closest island. They all used to swim back and forth to that island as kids.

Amy dropped what looked like a laundry detergent jug full of sand tied to a rope over the edge of the canoe, where it landed with a splash in the water and sank. Then she eased herself down to a seated position on the bottom of the canoe, flipped to a new page and started sketching. And still he continued to watch her, somehow unwilling to break away from her face, as her dazzling eyes scanned the world, her lips tilted up and her fingers moved.

Lord, please bring peace and happiness into her life. Help her find someone who will love her and Skye the way they deserve to be loved. Protect her from all of her enemies.

Jackson swallowed hard.

Protect her from the pain I'm now feeling and

from the foolish decisions I've made. Help me get justice for my sister and safety for Amy.

Then he dialed his boss.

"Jackson!" Finnick said. "How's Amy? Caleb just filled me in on what happened in the cottage last night."

Right, with everything else that had happened so far today, Jackson had forgotten to brief his boss on that part. Slowly Jackson started walking down the porch steps with Hudson by his side.

"She's okay," Jackson said. "Definitely a little rattled." Again, his eyes rose to the woman happily sketching in the canoe. "I didn't tell her that Gemma's body might've been found. And we have some privacy to talk without being overheard. Amy is incredibly strong, tough and brave. But I'm worried that she might be a little more shaken than she's letting on."

"Or maybe she's just pushing herself," his boss suggested, "and it'll all hit her later."

"Yeah, she's been hit with a lot." And now more bad news was coming. "I can't even remember what I've told you and what I haven't at this point."

"Well, let's go through everything now," Finnick said. "Top to bottom."

"It's a lot," Jackson said again. "Do you have the time?"

"I'll make time," his boss said. Jackson heard

him get up from his chair, say a quick word to someone that Jackson couldn't quite make out and shut his office door. A moment later Finnick's chair squeaked again. "Okay, I'm back. Again, I wish there was more I could tell you about the body that authorities believe is Gemma's. But we won't know more until the DNA tests are complete. And while our hands are tied on that, we can make headway in finding justice by talking through the case."

"Thank you." Jackson wasn't sure what he needed right now; he just knew that it didn't involve either staying still or being quiet.

He paced back and forth in front of the deck. He filled his boss in on the theory that whoever they were dealing with was a professional who had been clearly searching for something. He gave him a quick rundown of what had happened in the night and the mess they'd found when they got to the bookstore that morning.

"Sure, my immediate impression was that someone had trashed the shop," Jackson said. "But I don't think that he was intentionally trying to destroy the place. He didn't break anything. He just tossed it all on the floor, like he was looking for something."

"And you don't think he was looking for the hidden room?" Finnick asked.

"No," Jackson said. "Because he also opened

drawers. But Amy pointed out that none of the books were rifled through, so whatever it was couldn't have been small either. I'm guessing it's gotta be Gemma's laptop. Maybe she discovered something the Pine Crest killer wanted to make sure never saw the light of day."

He looked out over the water. Amy had tossed her head back and was laughing at something. He wondered what it was.

"Not a bad theory," Finnick said, dragging Jackson's attention back to the call.

"What are your thoughts on Gemma's cold case investigations?" Jackson asked.

He could almost hear his boss leaning forward in the chair.

"I'm familiar with a lot of them," Finnick said. "I'm not overly up to speed on the Pine Crest murders, but I'll definitely be digging into them and seeing what I can find. I've seen a lot of amateur sleuths in my time and your sister is head and shoulders above the rest."

"Well, Gemma has always been pretty driven." For better or for worse.

"You had no idea she was studying to get her private investigator's license?" Finnick asked.

"None at all," Jackson said. He could feel a touch of regret rising in his voice. He swallowed hard and tried to bite it back down. "I love my sister to bits, but we had very different personalities. As a teenager she found me annoying, in a really condescending way, and something about that made me want to annoy her more. Childish stuff, but we never worked through it. Because Gemma was the kind of person who avoided conflict."

"Like she'd give someone a fake name to avoid discussing the mistakes she made in the past?" Finnick said gently.

Touché.

"I think it's fair to assume that Gemma was heading to Pine Crest the day she disappeared," Jackson said. "I'm going to suggest I go there with Caleb to check it out, while Blake stays with Amy."

Not that he imagined Amy would be happy being left behind. But he wasn't about to take her into danger.

"What was Gemma's personal connection to the Pine Crest case?" Finnick asked.

"None." Jackson blinked. "Gemma didn't have any connection to that case."

He heard the sound of a small speedboat. A warning brushed the back of his spine. The masked intruder had escaped in a motorboat. Jackson scanned the lake but didn't see anything. He hadn't realized there was anyone else out on the lake. Not that the sound of a boat in itself was a reason to worry. He just hoped it wouldn't make waves and jostle Amy's canoe.

Just to be safe, he started toward the dock.

"It's just that normally when people are drawn so strongly to investigate a cold case like this, it's for a personal reason," Finnick said. "A lot of amateur detectives feel a very close relationship to their first case. Especially if it's one they're willing to risk their life for."

"Well, she does have a personal interest in a different cold case," Jackson said. "Her college roommate disappeared years ago and was never found. But that was a long time ago."

"And none of your family or friends were connected with Pine Crest?" Finnick pressed.

"Not that I can think of," Jackson said.

The sound of the boat drew closer. Instinctively, Jackson picked up his pace, readying himself to wave at whoever was driving and shout at them to slow down. A small speedboat raced past, cutting right in between the cottage and Amy, momentarily blocking her from view. A tall man stood at the wheel, his face hidden by a baseball cap. Then he was gone. The canoe rocked in his wake. Amy sat up straight and frowned.

"Nothing is ever truly random," Finnick said. "Like I said, I've heard of the Pine Crest case and I'll see what more I can find. But there has to be some reason she was heading there on that particular day. Maybe she found something specific, had a contact there or was meeting with someone."

The speedboat had turned around and was coming back again. Jackson hurried down the dock, with Hudson at his side. It was a long lake. Why come so close to the only other boat on the water?

Was it the same man from the night before?

"She hadn't completed her private investigator training or gotten her license yet, as far as we know," Finnick continued. "So, it's very improbable that she was hired by someone. She had a bookstore to run and a friend staying with her who's in need. And yet something pushed her to go there in person, without telling Amy. Why?"

The motorboat rushed back into view. Amy looked up. Her face paled. The boat was aimed straight toward her.

"One second," he told Finnick. "There's an aggressive boat out on the lake and he's hassling Amy. I'm worried he could be our intruder."

The driver took one hand off the wheel.

Then there was a flash of light, and a deafening bang shook the air.

Fear filled Jackson's core. The speedboat raced away. The smoke cleared.

The canoe had capsized—flipped over completely and lay upside down in the lake.

Amy was nowhere to be seen.

* * *

Amy surfaced under the feeble shelter of the overturned canoe and gasped for breath. White spots still blinded her vision and her ears rang from the flash bang. She furiously treaded water as her mind scrambled to process the past few seconds. The boat had drawn near again. She'd seen an unfamiliar man's chin and mouth underneath the brim of a hat that had been pulled down low. Then something long and cylindrical had glinted in his hands. Jackson's description of a stun grenade had flashed through her mind, and she'd thrown herself over the side of the canoe just as the man pulled the pin.

She closed her eyes and focused on trying to slow her shallow breathing and frantic strokes. Now what? She was still alive. Amy thanked God for that. The sound of the motorboat was fading in the distance. As it did, she could hear the faint sound of Jackson yelling her name, telling her to hold on and then commanding Hudson to help her. That was followed by what sounded like a splash.

Then she couldn't hear his voice anymore and the sound of water lapping up against the side of the overturned canoe surrounded her again. Okay, she was a strong swimmer and Jackson would come for her. True, it might take him a while to swim out this far, but she had told him where to find the keys to the neighbor's boat. All she needed to do was hold on and wait.

Then the sound of the small speedboat rose. It had turned around. The man who'd set off the stun grenade was coming back.

Help me, Lord. I can't stay here. But I don't want to risk swimming all the way back to shore either.

She opened her eyes and took a deep breath. The slightly acrid smell of the stun grenade's smoke still hung in the air. There was a tiny little island not far away. No more than a pile of uneven rocks punctuated by a few trees. She'd swim there, hide among the rocks, and Jackson could pick her up from there.

Suddenly, she felt a hard and insistent cramp fill her belly. It was sharp and so overwhelming, she heard herself cry out as the pain seemed to block out every other thought from her mind.

Help me, God!

She had to get to safety. Now. For Skye. That was all she knew for certain and it was the only thing that mattered.

Amy slid out from under the canoe on the same side as the island, so that the overturned canoe hid her from the view of the man on the approaching motorboat. She couldn't hear Jackson or even see the shore.

I have to hold onto my faith that Jackson's out

there, that I can trust him and that he's coming for me.

She fixed her eyes on the tiny island ahead of her and started swimming. Already her arms and legs were aching from the struggle of treading water, despite her life jacket. She'd always been a strong swimmer. But the added weight of carrying her unborn child seemed to drag her down and sap the strength from her body.

The sound of the boat roared closer. She was never going to make it in time. Would he hit her with another flash bang and cause her to drown? Did he have a gun? Would he run her over?

Amy swam on, pushing her pain-filled body through the water. Just a few more moments, just a few more strokes, and she'd feel solid ground beneath her again. But the island seemed to get farther away with every breath. A fresh cramp swept over her stomach. This one was stronger than the last, filling her body with such crippling pain she whimpered. It hurt to breathe. It hurt to move. She wasn't going to make it.

Then she felt a soft but insistent head buffeting against her arm. She looked over. Hudson was swimming beside her. Jackson must've sent the dog to help her while he ran for the neighbor's boat. The German shepherd pushed his snout against her hand repeatedly as if trying to get her to wrap her arm around his neck.

It's okay, his large brown eyes seemed to tell her. *Let me help you.*

She gasped a deep breath. Relief filled her core. She slid her arm around Hudson and grabbed ahold of his collar tightly. Together they swam for the island. She focused on the small patch of land ahead, trying to block out everything else but taking one strong kick after another.

Finally, she felt slippery rock underneath her feet. She climbed up onto the island on her hands and knees, with Hudson by her side. He licked her face. She hugged him. "Thank you."

She could hear the neighbor's larger boat now. The speedboat might take another pass at her, but she was safe on the island now and Jackson was on his way. It was going to be okay, no matter how many loud bangs and flashes of light the joker might unleash at her. Her palms pressed into the solid ground. She rolled over to a seated position and slowly inched her way up the rock. She could see the tiny speedboat on her left coming fast and beyond it, Jackson at the helm of their neighbor's stronger and more powerful watercraft.

Hudson positioned himself between Amy and the approaching speedboat. His hackles rose and his teeth bared. The man in the boat raised his hand again.

Her heart stopped. This time he wasn't holding another flash bang.

He was holding a gun. His boat slowed.

"You come with me or I shoot you!" the man shouted across the water toward her. "This isn't a game!"

The accent sounded even more fake than it had the day before. But his voice was no less menacing. His boat grew closer. So did Jackson's boat behind him, but he wouldn't reach her in time.

Hudson barked furiously. The criminal's boat drew so close it was only a few feet away. The man's finger brushed the trigger.

"You will get in the boat, Amy!" he shouted. "Now!"

With a growl, Hudson leaped at their attacker. The gun fired.

EIGHT

Time around Jackson seemed to move in slow motion, as he stood at the wheel of the neighbor's speedboat and watched as his faithful partner sprang through the air at the gunman, even as the criminal fired.

For a long, agonizing moment the sound of the bullet echoed around the lake, seeming to shake the air. Jackson heard the faint sound of Amy crying out in pain or terror.

Then Hudson landed in the gunman's boat. The bullet had gone wide and Hudson had escaped its path. The German shepherd clamped his jaw on the shooter's arm before he could fire again.

A prayer of thanksgiving rose in Jackson's heart, battling the sorrow and fear swirling within his chest. Gemma might already be gone. But he still had a fighting chance to get Amy and Hudson out of there alive.

His partner was now in the criminal's tiny boat, battling him. The gunman was wrestling with the dog, trying to force him to let him go. Amy was still nowhere to be seen, but still he could hear the plaintive sound of her crying. Jackson pushed the neighbor's speedboat as fast as it could go, but he was still so far away. Desperate prayers filled his heart.

Lord, please protect them. Keep Amy and Hudson safe.

Please help me reach them in time.

I might've already lost my sister. I can't lose anyone else today.

The rocky island lay ahead bare and empty. He watched as the criminal gave up trying to wrestle his hand free and started trying to use brute force and punch his partner in the face. But the German shepherd shook his head back and forth, dodging the blows. Jackson knew that Hudson wouldn't relinquish his grip until Jackson gave the order. Not as long as Hudson thought that Amy was still in danger and this man was going to hurt her. The attacker's small speedboat began to spin wildly in circles, threatening to capsize or run aground on top of the small island where Jackson could only hope Amy was sheltering.

Jackson's boat roared closer. He raised his hand, with the gun strong and steady in his grasp, knowing that unlike the man now fighting against Hudson, there was no way his shot would miss its mark.

"RCMP!" Jackson shouted at the top of his lungs. "Stop the boat now! Or I'll shoot!"

Suddenly the boat righted itself and began to speed away, taking Hudson along with it.

No, he was not about to allow this criminal to escape with his partner.

"Hudson!" Jackson shouted. "Release! Go! Swim to Amy!"

Immediately, the dog released his grip and leaped off the boat. Hudson began to swim back to the island. The small speedboat sped off and in a moment was gone from view. It seemed the man had seen Jackson coming and decided that dealing with both an RCMP officer and his K-9 partner was more than he'd bargained for. Relief filled Jackson's core.

Thank You, God.

Hudson reached the island just before Jackson did and scrambled up onto the rocks. Jackson slowed the boat to a crawl so he could stop safely without running aground.

"Amy!" he called. "Are you all right?"

"Jackson!" Her voice was faint and weaker than he'd ever heard it before. "I'm... I'm here."

Worry filled his core. She'd said "here." Not that she was okay.

Hudson disappeared behind an outcrop of rocks. Jackson cut the engine entirely, drifted up to the island and dropped anchor. Then he leapt off the boat and made his way across the slippery ground in the direction Hudson had gone. Finally he saw her. Amy was sitting on the ground, soaking wet and shivering. Her body was curled up in a protective ball, with her knees pulled up in front of her and her arms wrapped around them. Pain wracked her features. Her face was so pale, he thought she'd faint.

Hudson sat beside her, with his head held high, his ears alert and his body pressed up against her. The dog woofed softly in greeting but didn't leave Amy's side.

Good dog.

"Hey, Amy," he said, softly. "It's okay. I'm here now and I'm not going to let anything happen to you. Now, we need to get you in the boat and back to shore. Are you hurt? Can you walk?"

She looked up into his face. Anguish pooled in the depths of her eyes. Jackson's heart lurched.

"I think I'm in labor," she said. "The closest clinic is over an hour away…and Skye's coming now."

Time passed in a blur of fear and pain for Amy as Jackson gently helped her back into the boat and ferried her and Hudson to shore. He moored the boat at Gemma's dock. Then he scooped Amy up into his arms and slowly carried her back to the cottage as Hudson trailed them protectively.

She wanted to protest that she was capable of walking on her own but then felt the pain of another contraction rip through her body. She clenched her teeth and did her best to hide it, but somehow Jackson knew immediately.

"How many contractions have you had so far?" he asked.

"Five," she said. "Thankfully, that one wasn't as bad or long as some of the others."

She could feel her heartbeat beginning to slow, and the painful anxiety that clutched like a fist inside her chest started to loosen its grip.

Jackson climbed up the back steps carefully. Then he slid the back door open and they walked inside the cottage.

"Are they coming faster?" he asked. "Are the contractions getting longer?"

She shook her head. "No. They haven't been steady. Just painful and scary."

"Okay," he said, "right now we focus on keeping everything nice and calm, while I call 911."

Jackson laid her down gently on the couch, draped a blanket over her, and helped her out of her wet shoes and socks. Hudson parked himself on the floor in front of her defensively. Jackson pulled his phone from his pocket, and then carefully eased himself down on the couch under Amy's head so that she leaned back against his chest like a pillow. She hadn't even realized he'd grabbed a towel from his bag until she felt him gently running it over her sopping wet hair with one hand while he dialed with the other.

"Yes, hello." His voice was both steady and commanding. "My name is Jackson. I'm an RCMP sergeant." He rattled off a police badge number. "I have a twenty-eight-year-old civilian who's seven months pregnant—"

"Thirty-four weeks," Amy interjected weakly.

"Thirty-four weeks pregnant, with a history of high blood pressure and who's having painful and irregular contractions." He paused for a moment and seemed to be listening to the dispatcher. "We're in Clearwater, Ontario. Over an hour drive from the nearest medical clinic and a two-hour drive from the hospital in Huntsville."

Suddenly, pain swept over her again. She clenched Jackson's hand so tightly she could feel her nails digging into his skin. She'd have expected him to yelp in pain or push her away. But instead his thumb gently brushed against the back of her hand, as he glanced at the clock on the wall and counted the seconds as they ticked. Then the pain stopped and he filled in the dispatcher. There was a long pause as Jackson listened to whatever they were saying in response.

"We need to get in the truck and go," Amy said. "I'm not having my baby here."

"We don't want you having her on the side of the

road either," Jackson said, softly. "Thankfully, your contractions are uneven and we still don't even know if you're in active labor. If Skye is going to come into the world today, we're a lot safer here, in a nice warm cottage with running water and professional help on the line, then if there was some kind of emergency on the side of the highway."

Jackson leaned forward and she felt his lips brush against her temple in a comforting kiss.

"What I need you to do right now is focus on taking slow, calming breaths and seeing if we can get your heart rate down," he said, his voice barely above a whisper. "The fact the contractions are erratic and seem to be slowing down is a very good sign that this might just be false labor. The dispatcher is arranging for emergency medical help, and it might take an hour for them to get here. But I've got a paramedic on the line right now who's not going anywhere until we're sure you're okay. Right now, all you've got to focus on is resting and breathing. You're not alone. Hudson and I are here, and we're with you every step of the way."

Hudson nuzzled her hand. Then the German shepherd laid his head on the couch beside her belly as if reassuring both her and Skye that he was there. Amy tried to pray but was unable to put words to the cries of her heart, beyond calling out to God for her and her baby's safety.

"How can I help you?" Jackson asked.

"Talk to me," she said.

"About what?"

"Anything," she said. "Something lighthearted. Just distract me with something."

"Okay." She felt Jackson shift beneath her as he reached over the back of the couch for something on the shelf behind him. There was the gentle rustle of pages. Then he began to read.

The book was one of Ajay's old adventure novels, featuring the same mystery-solving brothers as the book she'd found the note in back in the camper. In all the chaos that had happened in the past few hours, she hadn't really given herself time to think about the fact that Gemma's brother had had feelings for her when they were younger. But now she could feel the memory of it fluttering in the back of her mind.

Jackson's voice began to rise and fall in a soft melodic cadence as he read. She closed her eyes and rested in the comfort of his arms, as his words moved around her. Time ticked past, her breathing slowed, the pain stopped and then she began to feel the gentle flutter of Skye moving inside her.

Eventually Jackson stopped reading. "Have the contractions stopped?"

"Yes, and Skye's kicking."

"Thank You, God," he whispered.

He glanced at the clock on the wall, then he shifted the phone to his ear, and she remembered that there'd been someone waiting on the line the whole time.

"Okay, it's been half an hour since the last contraction," Jackson said. "The baby's kicking. I think we are good. Yup, okay, I'll get her to eat something and then will drive straight there. Thank you so much. I really, really appreciate everything. And if anything changes, I'll call right back. Thank you again."

He hung up and set the phone down on the table.

"She's called off the paramedics," he said, "which is good because there was a major accident on the highway north of Huntsville and they're short-staffed. We've got an appointment at a medical clinic in South River. They're the closest place that has the kind of facilities to make sure you and Skye are okay. It's about an hour from here, and I'll take you there as soon as you're ready."

South River was also only fifteen minutes away from the Pine Crest Retirement Home and near where Gemma's car had been found.

"Emergency services have already contacted the clinic and let them know to expect us," Jackson went on. He slowly eased himself up from the couch and set a large pillow behind Amy's head for her to lean back on. Then he stepped over Hudson and started for the kitchen. "I'll also text my colleagues Caleb and Blake and ask them to meet us there. They're probably delayed by the accident on the highway, so they should arrive there around the same time we do."

She stretched slowly.

"Are we going to stop in at Pine Crest Retirement Home while we're in South River?" she asked.

"I am," Jackson said. He stopped and looked back but didn't quite meet her eyes. "Hopefully, I'll be able to find out why Gemma was heading there and what her interest was in the case. I'll take Caleb with me. But I think it's better that you rest."

She couldn't argue with that, even though part of her really wanted to go. But she couldn't exactly rest and play detective at the same time.

But I don't want you to leave me alone at the clinic. I want you to stay there with me!

The thought crossed Amy's heart. But she pressed her lips together and stopped herself from saying it.

Jackson wasn't her boyfriend or her friend—let alone her husband or someone who'd stepped up to take any responsibility to care for her and Skye. No matter how safe and comfortable she'd felt in his arms, he wasn't a part of her life. He was just a stranger and police officer who'd happened to be there and stepped up to help her.

So what if she was drawn to him? And if she admired his kindness and generosity? Or how quick he was to leap in and help her, or how attentively he listened? After all, she'd married Paul and he'd turned out to be a liar who broke people's hearts and tossed them away like garbage.

How could she ever trust her own judgment ever again?

"The paramedic said it's important you eat something," he said. "Do you still have a hankering for crackers and peanut butter? Or are you craving something else? I make a mean scrambled eggs."

"No to the eggs, thank you," she said. "But I've got some leftover macaroni and cheese in the fridge if you don't mind reheating it."

"No problem, milady." The cop doffed an imaginary hat and gave a slightly goofy grin. "Your wish is my command."

She felt a weak smile cross her lips.

Jackson's legs twitched as if he was about to turn and walk away. But instead he stood there, just outside the kitchenette, looking at her. Somehow her own gaze was locked on his green eyes, and neither of them looked away. Something deep moved through her core. It was a feeling she'd never felt before. This man had protected, sheltered, calmed and comforted her. He'd helped her through the scariest moments she'd ever known and it hurt to know he was about to leave her life.

But she had a habit of leaping into things without paying attention to where she was going. And maybe that was fine when booking last-minute travel arrangements, but the growing life in her belly told her it was no way to make decisions about anything that really mattered.

No, she could not trust her feelings for Jackson—or any man—right now. And maybe she never would.

"Macaroni and cheese would be great," she called, realizing she was repeating herself but finding her brain lost for words.

She watched as Jackson busied himself in the kitchen, heating macaroni and cheese for her and making a peanut butter sandwich for himself. Odd how he always moved so comfortably around the cottage. Putting dishes away the night before and getting different ones out now. Grabbing a random book and reading it.

It was almost like he'd been there before.

Had he? It was also strange the way he sometimes surprised her by knowing just a little bit more about her and Gemma than she'd have expected. An unsettling feeling tickled the back of her neck. Just how long had he been investigating Gemma? Had he been watching them? Had he been lying to her?

She watched as he pulled the macaroni from the microwave, stirred it, then spooned it into a bowl. No, Jackson was a good man. A nice guy.

He'd never given her any reason not to trust him. Her own broken heart and mind were just playing tricks on her.

She reached for the book he'd been reading, hoping the words would settle her mind just like it had when Jackson had been reading to her. Instead, her eyes caught the large blue letters scrawled inside the cover. They were in the same handwriting as the letter she'd found the night before.

Do not touch!
This means you!
This book is property of Ajay
aka Arthur Jackson Locke

Just like that she felt the blood freeze in her body, as a kaleidoscope of small random pieces that had been swirling around her mind suddenly coalesced into one solid picture.

Her gaze rose to the man behind the counter.

She looked past the beard, a nose that had once been broken and the green eyes no longer puffy with bear spray. She'd been both foolish and blind.

Jackson had been lying to her. Her heart hadn't learned a thing after Paul's betrayal but had instead led her astray again.

The man who had come to her rescue, kept her safe and promised to help her find her missing friend was Gemma's brother.

NINE

Jackson stepped around the kitchen counter holding a bowl of warmed macaroni and cheese in his hand and watched as the color drained from Amy's face.

"What happened?" He set the bowl down on the table in front of her. "Is everything okay?"

Oh no. Had she somehow figured out that Gemma might already be dead?

But Amy's lips curled as if she'd just tasted something wretched. She wasn't feeling a pain like the hollow one in his chest. She was angry.

"You're a real piece of work, you know that?" She pushed herself up to standing. Instinctively, he stepped forward to help her but the fury that glinted in her eyes like daggers told him to stay back. "You lied to me! This whole time!" Her voice rose. "You're Gemma's brother, Ajay!"

He opened his mouth to respond.

But she spoke before he could get the words out. "Don't you even dare deny it!"

"I'm not about to deny it!" Jackson said. His words flew out rapid-fire, in fear she'd run out of the room before he managed to get them all out. His heart was racing so quickly he almost felt dizzy. "You're right! I'm Gemma's brother. In all the chaos of the attempted kidnapping and bear spray, I momentarily forgot to tell you my name was Ajay, because everybody calls me Jackson now—"

"Ha! Jackson Finnick?" Sarcasm dripped in her tone.

"No, Jackson Locke," he said, "and I should've told you that the moment I ran into you behind the store yesterday."

"Yeah, you should have!"

"I know! But I panicked, and I've been winging it ever since," he admitted. "I was afraid that if you knew who I was, you wouldn't let me help you and you'd refuse to tell me anything about what happened to my sister. For all I knew, you might've bear sprayed me again and told me to get lost."

She pressed her lips together, as if she was about to fire back a retort and had barely managed to catch herself. Whatever she had been about to say, he was pretty sure it wouldn't have been good.

"Look, when I came up here to look into what happened to Gemma, I never expected to run into you," he said. His voice rose. But not like he was yelling. More like he was drowning and begging her to throw him a lifeline. "I didn't know you were living here and running the store for her. I paced back and forth in front of the store for ages trying to figure out what I was going to say when I walked in the door. Remember, the police officer who interviewed you initially thought you might be hiding something, and I was afraid you wouldn't tell me what I needed to know to find her."

"So, you lied to me because you were afraid I'd lie to you?" she asked. "You prejudged me and assumed I wouldn't forgive you for the dumb things you did when you were young, because you can't forgive yourself."

No. Maybe. That wasn't true, was it?

"I was afraid you'd feel like you had to choose sides between me and my sister," he replied, "and that as usual you'd choose her and that would keep me from finding her alive." And now it may be too late. "I always intended to tell you."

"When?" She crossed her arms. "When exactly were you going to tell me?"

He ran his hand over the back of his neck.

"Honestly? Just before we met up with Caleb and Blake, so you'd have somebody safe to leave with if you never wanted to see my face again."

She rocked back on her heels. Something softened in her gaze.

"You're so hard on yourself," she said. "All your talk earlier back in the bookstore about how you were such a terrible kid that you could never be a father is ridiculous. Yes, you were a troubled teenager, but I never thought you were irredeemable. Until I found out you lied to me, I was really impressed with who you were as a person. You were kind and thoughtful, and from what Caleb said, your colleagues think you're a really great cop." Then suddenly her words caught on her lips. Her eyes widened. "When I called your unit to verify your identity, Caleb lied to me about who you were, too!"

"Trust me—" Jackson raised his palms "—there's no big conspiracy here. Caleb was just trying to have my back."

"What about the other cop?" she said. "Blake?"

"Blake had no idea," he said. "She's a really wonderful officer. You can trust her."

Amy looked at him skeptically.

He searched her face and prayed that God would give him the right words to say. But Amy closed her eyes for a long moment as if trying to block him out.

"Thank you for heating the macaroni," she said. Her voice was so eerily calm, he almost wished she'd yell at him. "We need to get out of here and get to South River for my doctor's appointment. I assume Blake can bring me back here and fill me in on what you guys find out at Pine Crest?"

Jackson took a step forward. "Amy, you know you can't stay here anymore," he said. "Not after everything that's happened. I know the plan earlier was that Blake would bring you back here. But now, after the boat attack, it's pretty clear that it's not safe."

And the K-9 Unit didn't have the authority to grant round-the-clock protection to her indefinitely.

She opened her eyes.

"Maybe it's not safe here," she said. "Maybe I shouldn't come back here at all. But that's *my* problem to figure out, not yours."

He felt like thousands of words were floating unspoken in the air between them. Jackson wanted to apologize again and keep apologizing for as long as it took to get her to smile again. When he'd seen her through the bookstore window the day before, his heart had begun pounding just like it had back when he'd been a teenager. But what had started out as a crush had grown since then. He'd realized just how courageous, thoughtful and caring she was. He liked Amy— so much more than he'd ever liked anyone before. He wanted to tell her that he was nothing like Paul, the man who'd lied to her, hurt her, betrayed her and left her. He wanted to explain how embarrassed he was for his past and that she was the most incredible woman he'd ever met.

But instead, all he said was, "You're right, we need to get you to the doctor. I'll quickly pack up my stuff, take Hudson for a jog and meet you at my truck."

"Sounds good."

"Look, I know I made a lot of mistakes," he said, "and you have no reason to trust me. But I promise you that I will do everything in my power to protect you and keep you safe. And so will Hudson."

"I know." Amy nodded. "I honestly believe your heart is in the right place. For the record, I've never thought you were a bad guy, Ajay. Just one who sometimes made really lousy decisions, and who now apparently can't forgive himself for them."

Jackson felt a sudden lump form in the back of his throat. He gathered up his stuff, signaled Hudson to his side, then went for a walk through the woods around the perimeter, being careful to never let the cottage out of his sight. When they got back, he found Amy waiting by the truck with an overnight bag in hand. They exchanged a few stilted words of small talk as each checked if the other was ready to go, then the three of them got in his vehicle and he began to drive.

It would take fifty-three minutes to get to the clinic, according to Jackson's GPS. That would give them plenty of time to talk and straighten out what needed to be said. Maybe he could even find a way to warn her that he had heard something about Gemma, and that while he wasn't authorized to give her all the details yet, it wasn't good news. Something inside him ached to ensure she got the news from somebody who genuinely cared about her and Gemma.

Instead, the two of them sat in silence as the time on his GPS counted down like a slow and painful detonator to the moment that he would say goodbye to her, knowing he'd probably never see her again. He turned the radio on but didn't pay much attention to whatever was coming through the speakers. When that didn't help he prayed, feeling like he was the last person in the world to have the right to talk to God about anything, but not knowing what else to do.

When there was less than half an hour left on the GPS, he glanced over at Amy and realized she'd fallen asleep with her head against the window and her sweatshirt curled into the crook of her neck like a pillow. She didn't stir again until he pulled into the parking lot of the South River clinic. Blake was already there waiting for him.

She walked over and reached Amy's door, before Jackson could leap out of the vehicle, run around and open it for Amy. Blake had long, black hair pulled back into a French braid, the kind of distinct look that some called "stunning" and a confidence that put people at ease. Amy stirred slowly, as if waking from a dream far nicer than the reality they were in.

"Amy Scout?" Blake said. "I'm Constable Blake Murphy. Please, call me Blake."

Amy smiled. "Nice to meet you."

He watched as Blake helped Amy out of the car.

"Hi, Blake." He leaned forward. "Thanks for doing this."

"No problem," Blake replied. "Caleb will meet you at Pine Crest. He called ahead and they're expecting you. He says to tell you to stop and change into your uniform on the way. He thinks it'll help open doors."

"He's probably right."

She slid her arm around Amy and walked her to the door.

"Goodbye, Amy!" he called. "Take care."

But the words seemed so inadequate for what he was feeling, and when Amy didn't look back he realized that she probably hadn't even heard him.

Lord, please take care of her. Find someone to be her protector in the way I could never be.

* * *

Twenty-two minutes later, Jackson pulled up in front of the Pine Crest Retirement Home, having stopped at a gas station on the way to get both himself and Hudson dressed up in their navy blue RCMP K-9 Unit uniforms. Pine Crest was a large and sprawling brown building, with wings that branched out in multiple directions like an angular spider. It would've been completely unassuming, if not for the abundance of gardens that surrounded it, from well-tended flower beds to rosebushes and even vegetable allotments.

Caleb had parked his vehicle down at one end of the parking lot and stood beside it. His short blond hair and bright blue eyes gave the overall impression that he was more likely to be an actor portraying a rookie on some small-town television show than an actual cop. At least until people learned he ran on coffee and sarcasm.

"Good to see you," Caleb said, as Jackson stepped out of the car. "I've been here less than half an hour and I've already managed to start a commotion. I think every single resident in this place has spied on me through the window in the past half hour. They'll be relieved I'm finally stepping inside."

Jackson snorted, thankful that someone was giving him a feeble excuse to smile. He opened the back door of his truck, let Hudson out and then clipped his leash to the dog's official RCMP harness.

Caleb smiled at Hudson and ran his hand over the back of the dog's head.

"Well, look at you!" Caleb said to the German shepherd. "Just wait until they get a glimpse of you and they'll forget all about me and your grumpy human partner."

"Do I look grumpy?" Jackson asked.

"You look deflated," Caleb said. "I'm guessing you told Amy the truth?"

"No, she figured it out on her own."

Caleb blew out a breath. "You did say she was smart. Does she hate you now?"

"I think she hates us both, dude."

"Us?" Caleb's hand rose to his chest theatrically. "What did I do?"

"You covered for me," Jackson said. "Did Finnick tell you the news about my sister?"

Caleb's smile dropped in an instant as he clocked Jackson's face. Jackson had never been any good at hiding what he was feeling.

"No," Caleb said. "Did they find her?"

"Maybe," Jackson said. "External indicators of a Jane Doe match the known fact pattern, but DNA tests have not yet been run conclusively."

"Oh man, I am so sorry." Sorrow filled Caleb's face. "A close buddy of mine was murdered a couple of years ago, and they still haven't arrested the woman I know is responsible for it, for lack of evidence. It's rough."

"Thanks," Jackson said. "I can't really talk about it because I'm not authorized to brief anyone yet."

"Brief anyone on what?" Caleb ran his fingers across his lips to mime zippering them shut. Then he gave Jackson a quick hug.

"Come on." Caleb slapped him on the shoulder. "Let's go impress a bunch of senior citizens with our crime-fighting skills."

Jackson looped Hudson's leash around his wrist and the three of them walked to the front door. The door swung open automatically and they stepped into an open concept lobby. A large living room lay to their right, with every available chair filled with a silver-haired senior pretending not to watch them walk in.

A woman in a crisp tan blazer appeared and greeted them with a handshake.

"Nice to meet you, officers," she said. "I'm Marjorie Wilson, general manager of Pine Crest Retirement Home. How can I help you today?"

"Thank you for your time," Caleb said. "I'm Constable Caleb Perry. This is my colleague Sergeant Jackson Locke and his partner, Hudson."

"It's about time you guys showed up!" a male voice called from somewhere within the audience watching from the lounge.

"Walter—" Marjorie directed her voice to a large, mustached man in a baseball cap who was sitting in a green armchair "—the officers are here to help, and we need to help them do their job."

Walter harrumphed and crossed his arms. "Over a decade too late."

"It's been twelve years since Angela, Mitsy and Gordon died!" another woman added.

"That's Captain Gordon Donnelly!" Walter corrected. "He served in the Canadian Air Force!"

Various other seniors leaped into the conversation, their voices blending into a chorus.

"In the Second World War!"

"Mitsy Therwell had six grandchildren and Angela Jeffries knitted everyone scarves!"

"It was crochet, not knitting!"

Marjorie turned toward them and raised a hand. "Everyone, I'm sure the officers appreciate that you have strong feelings about what happened to our friends and will be happy to talk to everyone in turn."

"Tell them it was Kenny!" Walter shouted. "Everybody knows it was him!"

"Kenny?" Caleb asked.

"Kenny Stanton was a maintenance man at the time," Jackson said, "and a lot of people suspect he had something to do with what happened."

"But you cleared him!" Walter added. "Because he was sweet, charming and had a smile like he couldn't hurt a fly."

"*You* liked him too!" a woman yelled at Walter.

Walter ignored her and turned back to Caleb and Jackson. "Did you know the police took DNA samples and never tested them?" the man asked.

"No," Jackson said. "I didn't know that."

He glanced at Caleb. His friend's eyebrows rose.

"Is that true?" Caleb asked him in a low voice. "Did police bungle the case?"

"I don't know," Jackson admitted. "But I'm sure Finnick won't be happy to hear it."

"You know what it's like to have your friends die and no one cares?" Walter went on. "I wrote dozens of letters to every politician and newspaper in the country, for years, and nobody tried to help. Until that girl Gemma saw our social media posts about it and started messaging us. And now she's probably dead too."

Pain twinged in Jackson's heart.

Caleb turned from Walter and the chorus of senior citizen onlookers back to Marjorie. "Did Gemma ever come here?"

"No," Marjorie said. "She just conducted some phone interviews and exchanged emails with some of our residents. She was planning on coming here to show us some pictures the day she disappeared."

"What kind of pictures?" Jackson asked.

"I don't know."

"Kenny probably killed Gemma too!" Walter called.

A chorus of voices agreed with him.

"I'm sorry about all this," Marjorie said. "As you can understand, there's a strong feeling here that police haven't investigated the deaths of Mitsy, Angela and Gordon as they should have."

He thought of the wall of victims' faces in Gemma's hidden office. Did every one of them have family and friends who felt the police had failed them too?

For the next two hours, Caleb and Jackson interviewed every resident and staff member who was willing to talk to them about the investigation. Thankfully, it all went faster and more smoothly than expected. Once they got past the initial and understandable frustration that many of the residents felt, it turned out that a lot of them were keen fans of mystery novels and crime shows. They were absolutely delighted to help in any way they could, especially if it meant getting a chance to pat Hudson and tell him what a good and handsome boy he was.

But the sad truth was that Jackson and Caleb left without much more information than they'd arrived with, except for the tip that police had taken DNA samples that might not have been tested. Nobody knew what Gemma had been heading to show them the day she disappeared, what had happened to her or why she'd been looking so intently into the case.

"Well, I've never felt so motivated to solve a case while simultaneously feeling completely and helplessly unequipped to do so," Caleb said, as he and Jackson got back to their vehicles.

"Agreed." Jackson unclipped Hudson's leash and opened the back door for him. Then he pulled out his phone and called Blake.

"Hey, we're just leaving Pine Crest now," he told her when she answered. "How are things with Amy?"

"Not good," Blake said. She blew out a hard breath. "I'm taking Amy to the South River Motel to hopefully book her into a room. The doctor told her she can't leave town until they run more tests. Looks like there might be something wrong with the baby."

Amy looked out the passenger-side window as Blake pulled her RCMP cruiser up in front of the South River Motel. A sign in the front window said there were no vacancies, but she was under strict instructions from her doctor to rest and the next closest hotel was over an hour's drive away.

"Don't worry," Blake said. "I'll go inside, talk to them and explain the situation. I'm sure we'll find something. Do you want to come inside with me or do you want to wait in the car?"

Amy glanced up at the blue sky. The doctor's words swirled around her mind.

The test results are concerning. Rest up and try to relax. We'll run tests again tomorrow and then see where we're at.

"I'd like to sit outside, actually," Amy said. "If there's somewhere we can do that."

Blake paused for a moment. She had a serious face, framed by wisps of black hair that had escaped from her braid, and gray eyes with dark rings around the irises. She was beautiful in an unconventional way.

"Okay," Blake said. "I'll see what I can do."

The constable got out of the car and headed into the motel office. A quick moment later and Blake was back to let Amy know there was a large, secluded lawn out behind the motel, where Amy could stretch out and rest under the watchful eye of the security camera.

Blake pulled a soft, gray blanket from her trunk, Amy grabbed her bag and together they walked around to the back of the building, where they found a lush patch of green grass surrounded on three sides by dense forest.

"You going to be okay out here?" Blake asked.

"Absolutely," Amy said. "I need some time to think. Thankfully, I brought my sketch pad."

Blake spread the blanket on the grass and then offered her arm for support as Amy sat.

"Thank you." Amy stretched her legs out in front of her. "I'm sorry, I hate that I'm in this situation and I feel like I'm inconveniencing everyone."

"Don't worry," Blake said. "I've got a baby at home myself. He's turning one in the fall."

Yeah, but judging by the thin gold band on her finger, she wasn't facing it alone.

"My baby's father is a con artist who's run out on us," Amy said.

"I know," Blake said. Then she chuckled kindly and a different, warmer smile crossed her face. "And let me guess, you're beating yourself up about it?"

"Yeah," Amy admitted.

Blake laughed again and then crouched down beside her.

"Can I tell you a secret?" Blake asked. "My husband, Dustin, is currently AWOL from the Canadian military and there's a warrant for his arrest for desertion."

"You're kidding?" A sudden burst of sympathy flooded Amy's core. "I'm so, so sorry."

"Thanks," Blake said. She held up her phone and Amy looked down to see a picture of a clean-cut man with a big smile wearing a Canadian Army uniform. "I had no clue that Dustin had a drinking problem until after we were married. We got caught in this endless cycle of him apologizing and promising to never do it again, then I'd forgive him and it would happen again. Eventually, he joined the military, got deployed and told me it would be a fresh start." She sighed. "But he wandered off base, got drunk in a local bar and disappeared. So now I'm living with my mother, raising my kid alone and wondering if I'm ever going to see that sorry man again."

"I'm sorry," Amy said again, finding the words so inadequate for what she was feeling. Her heart twisted for Blake.

"Me too." Blake stood. "Just focus on that feeling of compassion in your chest right now, and practice directing that kind of love to yourself. We're all wounded by this world in different ways. So be kind to yourself and everybody else. I'll see you in a bit."

Blake turned and walked back around to the front of the motel. Amy sat in the sun and sketched. She hadn't been able to get the fleeting glimpses she'd seen of the intruder out of her mind. Maybe if she focused, she could find him on the page. Her fingers moved quickly. She hadn't been able to see the silent intruder's full face before he'd set off the flash bang back on the lake. But she'd been able to see his jawline and mouth. The day before, she'd seen his eyes

through the holes in his mask and she could make
a reasonable guess about the shape of his face.
Maybe if she put it all together, someone would
recognize him and know who he was.

Narrow eyes. Thin lips. Square jaw with an
otherwise long face.

But even as the stranger began to come together on the page in front of her, the doctor's
words still echoed in the back of her mind. Her
blood pressure had spiked. He'd wanted her to
rest locally overnight and come back in the morning for more tests. And if things still didn't look
good, she might have to find a place close to the
hospital in Huntsville and stay on complete bed
rest until Skye arrived.

She set the sketch pad down in the grass beside
her and ran her hands over her belly, feeling for
the comforting contours of her daughter's tiny
form. The baby stirred softly.

*Help me, Lord. I've never felt so alone. I don't
feel ready to be a mother and I'm terrified of fail-
ing her. Now my precious child may be in danger. I feel so alone and so completely helpless to
protect her.*

She heard the gentle jingling of dog tags. Amy
opened her eyes to see Hudson trotting through
the grass toward her in his official K-9 unit vest.
She looked past him and didn't see Jackson anywhere, but she knew he wouldn't be far away.

Hudson's tail wagged. He lowered his head as he reached her and nuzzled his nose against her arm.

"Hey, you." She ran her hand over his head. The dog licked her face gently then lay down beside her on the blanket. Amy buried her face in his fur and hugged him tightly.

Thank you, Jackson.

Somehow he'd known she didn't want to be alone right now, but had probably also figured that he was the last person she wanted to see. So, he'd sent Hudson to her on a solo mission. She lay down beside the dog for a long moment, feeling his heartbeat and resting in the comfort of having him there. Then after a while, Hudson's ears perked. The dog leaped to his feet. She sat up to see Jackson stepping around the side of the building.

He hesitated and seemed unsure whether to join them. Amy waved him over. Slowly, she sat up, cross-legged, resting her hands gently on her protruding belly.

"Blake told me I'd find you here," he said. "Caleb's with her now, waiting for the motel to sort out a room. Should be ready in a few minutes. They had someone leave early, they just hadn't cleaned the room yet."

"Well, I have something for you," she said. "I did a sketch of our silent intruder."

She nodded to the sketch pad that lay beside

her in the grass. He sat down next to her and looked at it.

"This is incredible," he said. "How did you figure out what he looked like?"

"I put it together from glimpses of what I'd seen," she said. "I don't know how accurate it is, but it's my best guess."

"Well, it's really good," Jackson said. "I'm going to send it to Finnick. He can assign someone to search the database for a match."

He held up his phone and took a picture of it. She heard the swooshing sound of the email sending. Then they sat side by side for a long moment, without either of them speaking.

She wanted to tell him that while she was still angry at him and didn't think what he'd done was even remotely okay, she believed he meant well. And she was glad to know there was someone on the case who cared about Gemma as much as he did.

"Blake said the doctor told you that you needed to rest and come back for more tests tomorrow?" he asked.

Concern creased his forehead. A deeper sorrow than she'd ever seen before pooled in his eyes.

"Yeah," Amy said. "My blood pressure is still too high. He's worried about the impact my ongoing stress will have on the baby. It's too soon to know for sure if I'm facing a more serious problem. But if I don't get better results tomorrow, I might be looking at complete and total bed rest until Skye is born."

Her voice hitched with an unexpected sob.

"Hey, it's going to be okay," Jackson said.

His hand brushed over hers then quickly pulled away, as if he'd just caught himself. But Amy grabbed his hand, even as he was pulling it back, and squeezed it tightly.

"I can't let myself think about medical stuff right now," she said. "Or I might fall apart. Please, I need a distraction. Tell me how things went at Pine Crest."

"Okay," Jackson said. Slowly their hands pulled apart. "First of all, Hudson was a really big hit."

Although the dog's head didn't turn, Amy couldn't help but notice Hudson's ears twitch toward Jackson as he heard his name.

"Turns out Pine Crest is full of the most incredibly vibrant and opinionated seniors I've ever met," Jackson said. "They are also extremely disappointed that the cops have failed to solve the twelve-year-old cold case of the deaths of three of their friends."

"I can't blame them," she said.

"Police took DNA samples that they might have never even tested," Jackson said. "Did you know that we don't have a dedicated cold case unit in Ontario? Finnick—my boss, Inspector Ethan Finnick, head of the RCMP's Ontario K-9 Unit—has been fighting for years for the creation of a single, multidisciplinary unit dedicated to solving cold cases. Which is something that exists in other parts of North America. He's as passionate about unsolved crime as other people are about hockey or baseball. Now it looks like Gemma was too."

She thought of the wall of faces and names in her friend's hidden office.

"These are cases that were never closed," he went on. "In some, families have no idea if their relatives are dead or alive. In others, they know they're gone, but it was never even determined if someone was murdered, died by accident or of natural causes." He sighed and leaned back on his elbows. "Sorry, I'm rambling."

"No, I asked for a distraction," Amy said. She lay back and looked up to the white clouds dotting a clear blue sky. "This is good."

"Well, I don't have any answers for the people at Pine Crest," he said. "Twelve years ago, there was a string of thefts. Then three elderly residents died of what may have been an accidental or intentional overdose of their pain medication IVs."

"What was stolen?" she asked.

"Umm…" He seemed to be thinking. "Well,

first of all, money. Everybody started missing cash, big and small. Then there was a lot of jewelry of varying value. Some gold coins. And a bunch of memorabilia from when Gordon served in the Second World War."

"And there's a suspect," Amy said.

"Yup, Kenny Stanton," Jackson said. "Charming guy, with brown or blond hair, depending who you ask. Everybody loved him and police initially cleared him. But when he didn't show up for work and dropped off the map, everybody became suspicious."

She glanced down at the face she'd sketched on her notepad. "I don't know if I'd consider him charming."

Jackson's phone suddenly pinged with a text notification. He sat up.

"Whoa," he said. "Maybe not, but your sketch did the trick. We now know who our silent intruder is."

TEN

"Are you serious?" Amy asked. "That was incredibly fast."

"Well, your picture was really good," he said.

She sat up and looked at the mug shot on Jackson's phone. The face that stared back at her was so close to the composite sketch they might've been twins.

"His name is Reese Cyan," Jackson read. "Age thirty-eight. Born in Ireland but moved to Canada when he was two, so his accent is definitely exaggerated. Long criminal record and several outstanding warrants for theft, breaking and entering, grand larceny, and trafficking in stolen property."

"Wow."

"But besides one minor assault charge, there's nothing violent on his record. Nothing like kidnapping or murder. He just steals stuff, sells it and also sells stuff that other people have stolen. So, whatever's going on here is a complete break in his pattern."

"He looks vaguely familiar," Amy said, "but I don't know for sure if I've ever seen him before."

"Maybe he was hanging around outside the bookstore?" Jackson suggested.

"Maybe," Amy said. "So, we have one answer and even more questions. Is Reese Cyan also Kenny Stanton? Did Gemma figure out he was behind the murders at Pine Crest?"

"I don't know." Jackson sighed. "I just wish Gemma had confided in me about all this. Maybe I would have let her down, but I just wish she'd given me the opportunity to be there for her."

"Well, you two were never close," Amy said gently. "She never talked about you or even told me you were now a K-9 cop."

Was that because Gemma was ashamed of her brother? Or because Amy was deep in the middle of a crisis and Gemma was hiding her own secrets? It was hard to judge a person's true thoughts and feelings by what got talked about in the middle of a hurricane.

"We actually used to be really close," Jackson said. "We were best friends when we were kids. People thought we were twins, because even though she was a grade above me, our classes were often combined."

"Really?" She'd had no idea.

"Everything changed when Gemma started grade seven and moved to a new school without me," Jackson said. "Suddenly she had this whole new life that I wasn't a part of and everything I did embarrassed her. She matured a lot faster than me. My parents were going through a divorce at the time, and I felt like everyone had forgotten I existed. So I got really loud and started doing stupid stuff to get attention. Figured being in trouble was better than being invisible." He ran his hand over his neck. "I'm not proud of it."

She thought of the note she'd found hidden in the camper. Part of her was glad he hadn't asked her out when they were teenagers, because she definitely hadn't been interested in romance back then. But maybe it would've been nice to be friends.

"I'm sorry," Amy said. "I never meant to take your best friend away from you. Everyone talked about how close Gemma and I were. Joined at the hip. Thick as thieves. I never intended for you to be left out."

"Well, it was pretty clear you hated me," Jackson said, quietly and without meeting her eyes. "Especially when you sent my letter back with 'I Hate You! Never Talk to Me Again!' written across it in huge block letters. Not that I blame you."

"I never did that!" Amy jolted upright. "You never sent me any letters!"

"Yes, I did," Jackson said. "I sent you one.

When I was fifteen. After I crashed your grandmother's car into the lake at your birthday party, I got arrested."

"I remember," Amy said.

Gemma had been so embarrassed of her brother. There had been dozens of cops. It had been chaos.

"I got probation," Jackson said, "and ended up in this special group program for kids with behavioral problems. It probably saved my life, and there were a lot of great people working there. But that's also how I got this dent in my nose. Some other kids were bullying me when we were doing our public service hours cleaning up trash, and the incredibly terrible cops guarding us decided not to step in, for reasons I can only imagine."

"I'm so sorry." Amy's hand brushed his arm.

"Thanks," he said. "Something about seeing both the best and the worst from people in law enforcement inspired me to become a cop and pushed me to pursue justice and rescue people for a living. They also had service dogs there, and they were just incredible. But I also think watching what I went through was another one of the reasons my sister doesn't really trust police. Gemma never understood how I could just forgive and move on. Despite our differences, she was really protective of me. Anyway, one of the steps I took was writing apology letters to everyone I harmed. My parents were in charge of passing them out. I wrote you one. Are you telling me you never got it?"

"No." Amy shook her head. "There's no way I'd forgot that."

Had Gemma intercepted it, pretended to be Amy and sent it back? Why would her best friend do something like that? Frown lines creased Jackson's forehead, and she was pretty sure he was thinking the exact same thing. But neither of them said it.

"I didn't hate you," Amy said. She stared down at the grass. "I liked you. At least until you started doing stupid stuff. I thought you were really cool, adventurous and smart. Maybe I even had a bit of a crush on you, and I wanted to get to know you better."

If she was honest, she had even more than a crush on him now. She was attracted to this man—for a dozen different incredible and wonderful reasons. But she couldn't even begin to trust what she was feeling, let alone act on it.

"Oh," Jackson said. "Well, I had a crush on you too."

"I know," she said. "I found a note you wrote hidden in one of your books in the camper."

"Wow." He brushed a hand through his hair.

"Just to be clear," she said, "I didn't like everything you did. I wasn't into people who pulled stupid antics. You became loud and obnoxious that summer you crashed the car. But I liked you before that. When you were the guy who carried adventure books around and were the only one brave enough to climb up onto the roof or jump off the highest rock in the lake. I liked that Ajay."

"So do I in retrospect," Jackson said. "I just wish I'd liked him back then."

His phone chimed with another text. Jackson glanced at it.

"Blake says your room is finally ready if you want to go lie down and nap," he said.

"Yeah, I probably should."

Jackson stood then reached for her hands; she took them and he helped her to her feet. They remained there a moment, face-to-face, with her fingers still linked in his.

"Again, I'm incredibly sorry for being stupid, both when I was younger and also yesterday," Jackson said. "But I hope you know that you're like a sister to Gemma. I know you're grateful for how she took care of you in the past few months. But if she were here right now, she'd tell you how thankful she is for everything you've done for her over the years. You were there for her when our parents were divorcing. And even though your lives took different paths, no matter where you are in the world, if she ever had a crisis—anytime, day or night—you'd answer the phone to be there for her. And she'd want to know that someone was taking care of you now."

He looked down at his hands enveloping hers. But somehow he didn't pull away, and Amy didn't either.

"I got some really bad news today when I was out on the porch talking to Finnick," he said. "I'm guessing you could tell."

"Yeah, you looked like you'd been shot," she said.

"Officially, I'm not allowed to brief you yet," he said. "Because we don't know anything for sure. But I don't want a stranger breaking bad news to you. And honestly, I'd rather get hit with a reprimand than hide something from you ever again."

She closed her eyes tightly as the worst thought she could imagine filled her heart. "Did they find Gemma? Is she dead?"

"Maybe," he said. "They don't know for sure, but they think it's possible. They found a Jane Doe they think is her."

Dread and pain washed over her in a cold, icy wave.

And he'd been keeping that news from her for hours? While he'd rescued her from the island, calmed her down when she was in labor and taken all the anger she'd unleashed at him when she'd found out he was Gemma's brother, he'd secretly been hiding the pain that his sister might be dead.

"Oh, Jackson. I'm so sorry."

She pulled her hands from his, wrapped them around his neck and hugged him tightly. He hesitated, then slowly embraced her.

"I want you to know that whatever you need, I'm here for you and Skye," Jackson said. "Just like Gemma would be if she were here. You are not alone. If you need me to help you find a place to stay until the baby is delivered, hire someone to live with you, or help cover your bills, I'm on it. If you want me to take time off work and drive you around, I will. Or if you want to avoid my grumpy mug altogether, we can find another way for me to help. It's up to you."

"Thank you." She hugged him tighter, as if they were both broken. Her head fell into the crook of his neck.

"You're not alone," Jackson said. "I care about you, I'm here for you and I've got your back. Whatever you need. I won't let you down."

She swallowed hard and gazed up into his handsome face. Sincerity filled his green eyes. Suddenly she wondered what their lives would've been like if they hadn't both made so many bad decisions.

His lips brushed against her forehead. Amy's

heart raced. Warning bells clanged in the back of her mind, telling her not to make the same mistakes she'd made in the past.

But she found herself tilting her chin up toward him.

Softly and gently, their lips met in a kiss.

Jackson was kissing Amy Scout. The most beautiful woman he'd ever seen in his life was in his arms, despite the fact there wasn't a shadow of a doubt in his mind that he didn't deserve her. And yet, her fingers were brushing the back of his neck, and her lips pressed gently against his in a gesture that was so tender and sweet, it made him feel both stronger and weaker than he ever had in his life.

Hudson growled, then started to bark furiously. Jackson heard the snapping sound of a footstep in the woods behind them. They weren't alone. Someone was watching them! Jackson and Amy sprung apart. He glanced to the tree line just in time to see a figure in a dark hoodie take off through the forest.

"Get behind me!" he shouted to Amy. He yanked out his phone and dialed Caleb.

"Hello?" Caleb answered before it had even rung once.

"We have a hostile," Jackson said. "In the trees

behind the motel. He's escaping on foot. I need you and Blake here now!"

"Copy that. On our way."

The criminal was running. But thankfully the woods weren't as thick as they were around Cedar Lake, and he could still catch a faint glimpse of the man between the trees.

Amy grabbed his arm. "You should go after him!"

"I'm not leaving you." Nor would he send Hudson without backup after someone who might be armed.

An instant later he saw Blake and Caleb sprinting around the corner of the motel, with their guns drawn.

"Blake, cover Amy!" Jackson yelled. "Get her to safety! Caleb, you're with me!"

He glanced at Hudson. His K-9 partner was standing at the ready.

"Go get him!" Jackson signaled his partner toward the departing figure. "Catch! Hold! Don't let him get away!"

Hudson dashed across the grass and into the trees.

Jackson glanced back at Amy, only to nearly be knocked back on his heels by the depth of emotion he saw in her eyes.

"Stay safe," she said.

"You too." Jackson turned and sprinted after

his partner, hearing Caleb just a few yards behind him. He ran through the woods, following the sound of Hudson barking as he pursued his target.

Lord, please help me catch him and finally bring this nightmare to an end.

Jackson pressed on, feeling fresh hope fill his core. Hudson would catch the suspect. This would all be over soon.

Sharp and furious barking rose ahead of him, punctuated by loud and frustrated snarls from Hudson that Jackson had never heard before when in pursuit of a suspect. Then the trees parted ahead of them and he saw why. Hudson stood on his hind legs at the base of a large pine tree. The dog's front paws hit the trunk again and again, as if trying to shake it hard enough to send his target tumbling to the ground. The suspect may have been trying to hide, but there was no way Hudson's keen senses were about to be fooled. The K-9 had him trapped.

"Hudson!" Jackson called. "Come!"

Immediately, the dog relented and trotted obediently back to his side.

"We have him cornered!" Jackson yelled back toward Caleb as the constable's face appeared through the trees. "Stay back and cover me!"

"Copy that!" Caleb shouted back.

Silence had fallen from the pine branches

above. Jackson pulled his weapon, steadied it with both hands and raised it.

"I'm Sergeant Jackson Locke of the RCMP's Ontario K-9 Unit," he shouted. "Drop any weapons and come down with your hands up!"

The branches rustled. Then pine needles rained down as a slight figure in a black hoodie dropped from above and landed in a crouching position with his hands raised.

"I'm arresting you on the suspicion of involvement in the murder of Gemma Locke and the attempted kidnapping of Amy Scout."

"What? Someone tried to kidnap Amy?" The figure tossed her head back, the hood fell from her face and Jackson's heart suddenly stopped beating as fierce green eyes every bit as determined as his own met his gaze. Jackson reholstered his gun.

He raised a hand to signal to Caleb without turning around.

"Stand down and go back to the others," Jackson called. "The suspect is my sister, Gemma."

ELEVEN

Jackson stood in stunned silence with his eyes locked on his sister's face. She ran both hands through her dark hair, in a gesture he recognized as one he did all too often himself, when he was trying to get his brain to think. Gemma had cut her hair short and spiky since he'd seen her last. It suited her. Despite all the terrible fears that had filled his mind, she looked strong and healthy.

"Okay," Caleb's voice came from somewhere behind him. "I'll head back to the others and let you handle it."

"Don't brief them!" Jackson shouted, suddenly. "Keep this between us."

He didn't want Amy knowing that Gemma was still alive until he understood what was going on.

"Got it."

He heard the sound of Caleb retreating through the woods.

Jackson stood there, speechless, and looked at his sister.

"I thought you were dead," he said.

"I'm sorry," Gemma said. "What happened to Amy? You said someone tried to kidnap her."

"Yes," he said. "A very scary masked man we now know is named Reese Cyan. Amy got away and she's fine, except for some worries about how her blood pressure will impact the baby. Reese broke into both your store and the cottage. He was apparently looking for something. But, as important as all of that is, I've spent the last few hours believing you were dead! Police dredged up some body downriver from where your car was found. They thought it was you."

A dozen different feelings bounced around inside him like popcorn sizzling in hot oil—relief, frustration, confusion, anger, joy—and he didn't know which one would fly out of the pot first.

"Why were you hiding in a tree like that?" Not the most important question, he knew, but the top one on his mind. "Why did you run from me? Why would you let me keep believing you were dead?"

"I came here to talk to you!" Gemma said. Now they were both almost yelling. "I didn't know you thought I was dead."

"How did you know where I was?"

"The Pine Crest seniors were posting all over social media that you and your colleague were just there asking them about the cold case," she said. "I tracked your truck to the motel. I was hiding in the woods to make sure the coast was clear and that none of the other cops would see me, and next thing I know my brother is kissing my pregnant best friend!"

His big sister's hands snapped to her hips, as if she'd caught him doing something wrong. He crossed his arms in response. He still didn't know what he thought of his fleeting kiss with Amy. He suspected it had probably been a mistake. She was in a really vulnerable place and he couldn't let it happen again. But that didn't mean he was about to let his sister give him grief about it.

"I decided to make a hasty retreat and come back later when you were alone," Gemma went on, "then next thing I know you've ordered your big, scary dog to chase me and take me down. Plus, your colleague was running after me too. So, of course I ran."

He looked down at his partner. Hudson was sitting harmlessly by his side, with his head cocked as he was trying to figure out what Gemma was saying about him.

"Do you think we can trust Caleb?" Gemma asked.

"Do I think we can trust *Caleb*?" Jackson repeated. "Yes, he's a good cop, and I trust him with my life. In fact, I gotta say I trust him a lot more than I trust you right now. Why did you disappear and leave Amy all alone like that? She was in trouble. She needed you! Why haven't you reached out to anybody in weeks?"

Words tumbled out of his mouth so quickly he could barely contain them. But then he caught himself. *Forgive me, Lord.* It didn't matter how upset he was or how justified those feelings were. All he was doing now was repeating the same old patterns and pushing her away. Jackson held up both hands, palms up, in a sign of peace.

"I'm so sorry." His voice dropped. "That wasn't fair to barrage you like that. I was just really scared that I'd lost you and that I'd never see you again. I kept telling everyone that you were so strong and tough, I was convinced you were alive, but…"

His words trailed off as his voice broke.

He watched his sister's lips quiver and thick tears fill her eyes. Wordlessly he opened his arms and stepped toward his sister. She threw her arms around him and hugged him hard. He hugged her back just as fiercely.

"I'm sorry you thought I was dead," Gemma said. "That sucks and I can't imagine how much that hurt."

"It hurt a lot," Jackson said. "Are you okay?"

She nodded. Then Gemma pulled back and he let her go.

"I thought I was doing what I needed to do

to save Amy's life," she said. "A stranger tried to kill me. I figured as long as he thought I was dead, I could hide out and figure out who he was and get the evidence I needed to stop him."

"But if he thought you were still alive, he might come after Amy?" Jackson asked.

"Yeah," Gemma said, "especially if I tried to return to normal life back at the cottage. If I was there with Amy, she'd be in the line of fire and she had nowhere else to go. And considering how the cops bungled the Pine Crest case, I couldn't dismiss the possibility there was a corrupt cop involved. If so, maybe contacting you would put you in danger. So, I thought it was safer for everybody if I sorted it out on my own."

Okay, he got that to an extent. But didn't she see why that had been the wrong thing to do? She never should've tried dealing with this alone. As relieved as he was to see his sister again, he felt like he was at risk of falling into the same argument he'd had with her a dozen times before. He got the desire to protect Amy. But she still should have come to him for help, even if there had been a corrupt cop involved in the Pine Crest murders. It's not like he couldn't take care of himself...

Just like she was certain she could take care of herself.

Gemma was always a very private person. Amy's words from the night before filled his mind. *She was the kind who'd avoid conflict at all costs...* Then another thought crossed his mind. *Maybe we're more similar than I'd like to admit.*

He glanced at the trees above and prayed.

Lord, I lost my sister once. I don't want to lose her again. Help me break the cycle. Help me to stop being a brawler and start being the peace-maker she needs me to be.

He ran both hands through his hair, then caught himself and realized he'd just mirrored what she'd done earlier.

"Why did you go to Pine Crest today?" Gemma asked.

"We found your hidden office in the store," he said. "It's incredible, by the way. Amy saw the Pine Crest folder on your desk and figured out that might have been where you were going the day you vanished. I'm so proud of you for going for your private investigator's license. I'm sorry you felt like you needed to hide it from me."

"I wanted to wait until I'd actually passed my test and had my feet under me," she said. "I thought if you teased me or argued with me, I'd be too full of self-doubt to go for it. And I was afraid you'd take it personally, like I was decid-ing to go a civilian route to somehow spite you when you were in law enforcement."

He laughed as heat rose to his face. "Well, to

be fair I did think something like that," he said. "But only for a moment, before I kicked myself for thinking it."

She laughed too. "I was hoping to take the test a few months ago, actually," she said, "but when Amy showed up she was so frazzled and upset. Then she got sick because her blood pressure was too high, and I didn't want to add to her stress levels."

"Yeah, I get that," Jackson said. "What happened to your car?"

"I was looking into the Pine Crest cold case," she replied. "I'd been doing a lot of online searches and sending emails, and I thought I had a potential lead. But while I was on my way there, a van ran me off the road. I barely managed to get out of the car before it went over the edge. It was terrifying. But thankfully I was able to escape with my bag and wallet."

She shuddered at the memory.

"I hid in the bushes for what felt like forever. The driver pulled over and started looking for me. He had a gun, and I was sure he was going to find me and put a bullet in me. But then he called someone, and I heard him tell them I was dead. I booked a nearby rental cottage, through an online app and under a false name, and have been hiding out there ever since."

He pulled his phone from his pocket and held

up the picture of Reese Cyan. Gemma glanced at the screen, and before he could even ask the question, he watched as his sister's face turned ashen.

"That's him!" She pointed at the screen. Her finger shook. "That's the man who ran me off the road."

"He wasn't wearing a mask?" Jackson asked.

"No." She shook her head. "His van had tinted windows and when he was searching for my body, he didn't bother to hide his face, either because he figured I was dead or he was planning on killing me. Who is he? Is he the real Kenny Stanton?"

"I don't know if he's Kenny," Jackson said. "He might've changed his name or used an alias. His name is Reese Cyan, and he's a thief and fence with a history of trafficking in stolen goods. He may have robbed Pine Crest and accidentally killed Mitsy, Gordon and Angela. Or been working with an accomplice on the inside at Pine Crest, we really don't know. He's the one who tried to kidnap Amy."

"You said he was looking for something," Gemma said.

"Yup," Jackson said. "Something bigger than a book and smaller than a secret room. So, our best guess is that he's looking for your laptop with all your files and research on it."

"Well, then joke's on him," Gemma said. "It

was destroyed when my car went into the river. It might as well be a brick."

A cold breeze cut through the trees. The sun was beginning to dip lower on the horizon. He couldn't stand out in the forest talking to his sister forever. They had to figure out where to go from here.

"I'm sorry that we haven't had the kind of relationship where you felt safe coming to me with whatever you were going through," he said. "I know we haven't always seen eye to eye. But I love you, I respect you and I promise that I'm going to do a better job listening to you from now on."

"And you're not going to sideline me and take this over?" Gemma said.

"No way," Jackson said. "I'm just glad you're safe, and I promise that no matter what I'll do everything in my power to protect you."

"Ditto," Gemma said.

He chuckled.

"Come on," he said, "it's time for you to go talk to Amy."

The motel room that Blake had arranged for her was simple, but nicer than Amy had expected. There were soft blue-and-orange patchwork blankets on two twin beds and a large portrait of a waterfall on the opposite wall above the television.

Amy lay on the bed closest to the door, on top of the blankets. Her eyes traced patterns in the white stucco ceiling as she tried to relax and remind herself that Blake was standing guard outside her door. Yet, with every beat of her heart, her mind filled with questions about Jackson.

Was he okay? Was he safe? Why had Caleb come back without him? Why wouldn't he give her an answer about where Jackson was now?

And above all, why had she kissed Jackson like that? She'd gotten swept up in the emotion of the moment. She couldn't let herself act impulsively. Not like that. Ever again. Not after the mistakes she'd made.

Finally, after what felt like an eternity, there was a gentle knock on the door.

"Amy?" Jackson's voice was soft. Her heart leaped at the sound of it. "It's me."

She sat up. "Are you okay?"

"Yeah, I'm great," he said.

"Come in," she said. "Blake has a key."

"Okay," he said. "But I've got some pretty big news. It's good news, but still I don't want your heart rate skyrocketing. So, I need you to take a really deep breath and let it out slowly. Okay?"

"Okay." She did as he asked. "I'm good."

The door opened gradually and there stood Gemma.

A cry slipped from Amy's lips. Tears of joy

filled her eyes. She swung her legs over the side of the bed as Gemma hurried across the room toward her. The two women hugged tightly, and Amy felt both relief and joy bubbling up inside her heart.

"I'm so sorry," Gemma whispered. "I never meant to scare you like that."

"I'm just glad you're still alive and that you're okay."

"Me too."

Finally, they pulled apart and Amy wiped her eyes. Tears shone in Gemma's eyes too, and although her friend's smile was wide, Amy couldn't help but notice the worry lines that creased Gemma's forehead.

"I never used to cry," Amy said, with a laugh, "but now it seems like I've been making up for a lifetime's worth of tears."

She glanced past Gemma to where Jackson and Hudson stood in the doorway.

"I'll leave you guys to it," Jackson said.

He started to close the door, but Amy reached out her hand toward him.

"Stay," Amy said, "and we can all talk this out together."

Jackson paused. He glanced at Gemma, and the siblings exchanged a long and indecipherable look.

"No," he said. "I've got to fill Blake and Caleb

in on what Gemma told me, and also call Finnick and loop him in. I might be a while. You two will be fine on your own. One of us will be guarding the door at all times."

He left and closed the door behind him.

"Seems like you two have gotten really close," Gemma said.

She walked over to the bed beside Amy's and sat down.

"Well, he came up to Clearwater looking for you," Amy said, "and had my back when a really scary guy broke into the cottage and the store looking for something."

"While we were walking back through the woods, Jackson filled me in on everything that you've been going through in the past couple of days," Gemma said. "Reese Cyan is the man who ran my car off the road. I hid and let him think I was dead because I wanted to protect you. I'm so sorry. I never thought he'd come after you."

"He was looking for something," Amy said, "probably your laptop so he could erase any of the evidence you'd collected on him."

"Yeah, Jackson told me that too. But my laptop is useless, so whatever he's after is gone."

Amy wondered if Jackson had told Gemma how he'd hidden his identity at first, given Amy his boss's last name and how she'd caught him. Normally, it was the kind of juicy gossip she'd have been in a hurry to share with her best friend. But somehow, Amy found herself hoping that Jackson hadn't told Gemma. He'd made a mistake. And despite all the time she and Gemma has spent giggling over his mistakes when they were kids, she really didn't want to make fun of him now.

I guess I've forgiven him, Lord. Help me forgive myself for my own mistakes too.

Gemma leaned back against the headboard, pulled her knees up to her chest, wrapped her arms around them and looked at Amy, just like she had countless times before during sleepovers when they were kids. Amy leaned back against her own headboard, wedged a pillow behind the small of her back and crossed her legs.

"I know you must have a lot of questions," Gemma began. "There's so much I need to tell you, and I owe you a pretty big apology too. But I don't want to get your blood pressure up or cause any problems for you and the baby." Gemma waved one hand toward her. "Especially after Jackson told me about the medical tests and bed rest."

"It's okay," Amy said. "But when my heart was racing before, it really helped when Jackson just calmly talked to me."

"My brother talked to you calmly?" Gemma asked, skeptically.

"Yeah." Amy laughed. "He's not always loud, like he was when he was a kid. I mean, he shouts really loudly when he needs to. But he's a really chill and cool person, actually. Did he tell you I went into false labor earlier today?"

"No." Gemma's eyes widened. "Are you okay?"

"It was pretty scary," Amy said. "But he held me and calmed me down, and then he read to me for half an hour. I think as long as our voices are calm and we're taking things in bite-size chunks, it would be good to hear everything you've been going through."

Gemma shook her head as if she had water in her ears. "Okay… I'll take your word for it. Just let me know if it gets too much."

"I will," Amy said. "Let's take it nice and slow."

Amy leaned back and listened as Gemma filled her in on her dreams of becoming a private investigator—how she'd gotten interested in cold cases when her college roommate Louise had disappeared, how that case had made her realize just how many unsolved crimes were at risk of being forgotten, how she'd set up the hidden office and started looking into the Pine Crest murders.

Even though Amy had the impression her friend was still hiding things from her—maybe to help keep her stress level down—there was something comforting about lying there and listening to her friend's voice rise and fall as if they were telling stories back in the cottage when they'd been kids. Gemma explained that she'd been studying to be a private investigator and setting up her office before she invited Amy to stay. But she didn't tell her because she hadn't wanted Amy to think she was being a burden or feel any additional stress or guilt.

"I didn't want you to think that you were getting in the way of my dreams," Gemma said. "You were already dealing with so much, you felt like you had nowhere else to go, and I didn't want to add anything onto your plate."

She kept talking, skimming over the details of being run off the road by Reese Cyan as lightly as a rock skipping over the surface of the lake.

"When I realized that Reese thought I was dead," Gemma went on, "I thought it would be much safer for you if I let him believe he'd killed me and then I could try to investigate this on my own."

"You were wrong," Amy said.

"Yeah, I see that now." Gemma sighed. "I honestly thought I was protecting you."

Amy didn't know what to say to that. For a long moment, both friends stared forward at the picture of the waterfall in silence. Maybe their friendship was always heading to a point like this. Obviously, Amy hadn't predicted something this dangerous and dramatic. But maybe this was what happened when everybody was so busy trying to protect each other and avoid conflict, they let things build up for weeks, months or years. Until finally, things blew up, just because they'd been afraid of hurting each other.

"I want you to know that whatever happens next, you and your baby can count on me," Gemma said. "We'll make whatever modifications needed so that the cottage is a safe place to rest and recuperate. Or if the doctor thinks the cottage is too far away from the hospital, I'll close the store and we'll rent a place together in Huntsville. Whatever it takes, it's going to be okay. You and me are in this together."

And where would that leave Jackson? Would he be shut out again, like they'd shut him out when they were younger?

"Thank you," Amy said. "I love and appreciate you more than I have words to say. But we're not kids anymore, right? We're not going to freeze your brother out this time?"

Gemma broke her gaze and didn't answer.

"Jackson and I figured out that you must've intercepted the apology letter he sent me when we were teenagers," Amy went on. "You scribbled on it that I hated him and never wanted to see him again."

Now a flush rose to Gemma's face. "Yeah, I'm sorry."

"I know you tried really hard in the past to protect me from Jackson," Amy said. "I know that you pushed him away when we were kids and didn't let him hang out with us, because he was obnoxious and loud. But your brother has grown into a different man since then. He's a good guy with a great heart and he means well—"

"I know." Gemma crossed her legs in front of her and leaned back in a posture mirroring Amy's. "I love my brother. But the reason I didn't talk about him when you moved back in with me, and the reason I sent his letter to you back like that, wasn't because I was trying to protect you from him. It's because I was trying to protect my brother from you."

Amy felt her eyes widen. "You were trying to protect your brother from *me*? Whatever made you think you needed to protect Jackson from me?"

"Because my brother might've had some problems as a kid," Gemma said. "But he also has a really soft heart—the biggest of anyone I know." She waved her hands in the air as if summoning a chorus of memories. "He cares deeply about people, and he's always had feelings for you."

She ran both her hands through her hair.

"And, Amy, you know how much I love you and value you," Gemma went on. "But you're spontaneous and a risk-taker. I like that about you. But I've always been afraid that my brother would give you his heart and you would trample over it on the way to your next adventure. I saw you kiss him today. I just hope you guys aren't making a big mistake getting close."

"You saw that?" Amy asked.

Of course, she should have realized that Gemma had been the one eavesdropping on them from the trees. But she'd been so distracted by having her long-lost friend suddenly turn up, she'd momentarily forgotten. Maybe the kiss had been a mistake and Jackson deserved somebody more steady and less impulsive than she had a history of being.

"Yeah, I was eavesdropping on you," Gemma said. "I was trying to figure out who all was at the motel with you and when I could risk coming out without being seen. For all I knew, one of the cops you were with was involved in covering something up in the Pine Crest case." She paused, then said, "Or maybe, if I'm being incredibly honest, maybe that's how I was rationalizing the fact I was thrown by seeing the tenderness between you two, and I was feeling frozen by indecision."

Gemma changed the subject and went on to tell Amy about the cottage she'd been staying in for the past few weeks and her failed attempt to figure out who Reese was. She explained that while she had never planned to hide so long, the more the days ticked past, the harder it was for her to figure out what to do.

After a while, Amy felt her eyes begin to close, and she realized she was drifting. Gemma gave her another hug and slipped out, promising she was going to talk to Jackson, but she'd return soon. Gemma locked the door behind her and Amy heard her say hello to Caleb, who she assumed must be standing guard.

Amy didn't expect to fall asleep, but somehow she felt her eyelids grow heavy. She lay back on the bed against the pillow, wrapped a blanket around her and closed her eyes.

She started to pray, thanking God that Gemma had been found alive and safe, and asking God to keep Skye strong. Then she started to tell God how thankful she was for Jackson. She fell asleep with the memory of his face filling her mind.

She awoke to the sound of a high-pitched beeping. She sat up and swung her legs over the side of the bed, feeling suddenly light-headed. The sun had set outside the window. The motel door clicked and swung open, and Caleb rushed in.

"We've got to go!" Caleb said. "Somebody's set off the fire alarm."

She gasped. "I don't smell smoke."

"It might be an attempt to either lure you out or get to you in the chaos." He reached his hand toward her. "Come on, any second now and the parking lot is going to be full of people and emergency vehicles."

She shoved her feet into her shoes and crossed over toward the door.

"Where are Jackson and Gemma?" she asked.

"They're on their way to Pine Crest with Hudson," he said, "to show everyone the picture of Reese and see if anyone recognizes or identifies him as Kenny.

"Blake had to go back to Toronto," he added, "so it's just me for now." Caleb held up his phone. "But I'm calling Jackson right now."

Caleb put the phone on speaker and pressed it into her hands. She stepped outside. The fire alarm seemed even louder out in the parking lot. Motel guests streamed out of their rooms. Sirens wailed in the distance.

"Hey, Caleb," Jackson's voice came on the line. "Just on our way to Pine Crest."

"Jackson," she said. "It's me."

Caleb took her arm gently and steered her through the busy parking lot to the end of the building.

"Amy!" His casual tone shifted to concerned in an instant. "Are you okay? Where's Caleb?"

"I'm here!" Caleb called. "Someone set off the fire alarm so I'm evacuating Amy to safety."

"I'm fine," Amy said. "This place is turning kind of chaotic right now."

"Gemma and I are on our way," Jackson said. She could hear the tires screech through the phone. "We're turning around now and should be there soon. You there, Caleb?"

People kept streaming into the parking lot. Amy handed Caleb the phone. They pushed through the crowd, like fish trying to swim against the current.

"I'm here!" Caleb confirmed.

"Get Amy out of there," Jackson said. "Put her in your car and drive north. We'll meet up with you en route and find a quiet place we can touch base away from the chaos. Keep the line open."

"Will do!" Caleb said. He dropped the phone to his side, but she noticed he didn't end the call. "My vehicle is parked around the side. I didn't want the fact an RCMP SUV was parked in front of the motel to alert anyone to your location."

But maybe someone had found her anyway.

Fire trucks and ambulances began to pull into the front lot. He led her around the side of the building where a lone white police vehicle sat beside a thick wall of trees.

Caleb opened the side door for her.

"Don't worry." He smiled. "Everything is going to be okay."

She heard the sound of the gunshot before she could even determine where it was coming from. Caleb's face went ashen; he clutched his chest, then crumpled to the ground in front of her. His phone fell. Blood seeped from the wound between his fingers.

Amy screamed.

"Caleb!" Jackson shouted. "Amy!"

Then a masked man stepped out from the trees. He aimed a gun directly between her eyes.

"Don't move," Reese said. "Don't move a muscle! You are going to get in the car and we're going to take a little ride. Otherwise, I will kill you and your baby."

TWELVE

"Amy!" Jackson shouted her name into the cell phone that was mounted on his truck's dashboard. "Caleb! Update!"

But all he could hear was the muffled sound of a man shouting, a door slamming and then an engine revving.

"That sounded like a gunshot," Gemma said.

He glanced over at his sister, who was sitting in the passenger seat of his truck. All the color had drained from her face.

Then the call went dead. The highway stretched long and endless ahead of them. They were still a good fifteen minutes away from the motel.

Dear Lord, please help me get there in time. Please keep Amy, Caleb and the baby safe!

Hudson whined in the backseat, and Gemma reached back to comfort him.

Jackson dialed 911.

"Emergency services." The male voice that answered sounded confident.

"This is Sergeant Jackson Locke of the RC-MP's Ontario K-9 Unit. Reporting sound of a gunshot at the South River Motel. Possible officer down, named Constable Caleb Perry. Potential injury or abduction of a pregnant civilian named Amy Scout."

"Are you on the scene?" the dispatcher asked.

"Negative," Jackson said. "I'm on the road about fifteen minutes away. I was on the line with Constable Perry when it happened."

"Are you still?"

"No," Jackson said. "Call went dead."

He heard the sound of a keyboard clacking down the line. Gemma sat back in her seat, leaned over and squeezed Jackson's arm for a long moment.

"The sound of gunfire was called in by several people on the scene," the dispatcher told him. "Police are converging. Search and rescue helicopters are being deployed. Constable Perry was found alive with a gunshot to the chest and is being tended to. But the civilian, Amy Scout, was not found. It is believed she was abducted by the gunman in the officer's vehicle. The vehicle was last seen headed west. Officers are mobilizing roadblocks."

He glanced quickly at Gemma because it sounded like she was struggling to breathe. He knew it was caused by her worry. He knew the feeling. Fear seized Jackson's heart so tightly his head felt dizzy. But he took a deep breath and prayed.

Lord, help me focus. Amy needs me to think like a cop right now.

Not like a man who could lose a woman and child that his foolish heart longed to hold.

"The suspect may be a man named Reese Cyan," Jackson said. "RCMP Ontario can provide officers with a picture. He is a suspect in a crime that we're investigating."

More keyboard clicks and clacks. Jackson wondered how many people the 911 dispatcher was coordinating with right now.

"The suspect won't stay in the RCMP vehicle for long," Jackson said. "He'll have some alternative getaway car hidden out of sight that he'll switch the hostage into."

But he probably hadn't been expecting to come up against an officer who knew the rural roads of Northern Ontario like the back of his own hand, as Jackson did.

"I'm going to keep the line open and try to cut him off," he added.

"I can't advise that," the dispatcher said.

"I know," Jackson replied. "Huge thanks to you and everyone else working to get her back safely."

Then Jackson glanced at Gemma. His sister's worried eyes met his.

"Hold on tight," he told her. "I'm going to go

off-road, do a bit of fancy driving and see if I can cut Reese off. You might want to grab the phone in case it goes flying."

Then his eyes cut to the rearview mirror and he glanced at Hudson in the backseat.

"Sorry, buddy," he said. "I know how much you hate wearing your seatbelt. But if you'll be patient with Gemma, I'm going to get her to buckle you in."

Thankfully the dog was still in his K-9 vest and harness. Jackson glanced at his sister.

"On it." She'd already taken her seatbelt off and was squeezing her torso between the two front seats to reach the dog.

"It's the long, gray seatbelt to the right," he said. "Just feed it through the thick loop at the front of his harness, and buckle it in."

"I got it!" she called. He heard a click. Then Gemma refastened her seatbelt and grabbed his phone off the front console.

"Ready?" he asked.

Gemma took a deep breath. Then she gritted her teeth. "Ready."

His sister sounded even more determined than he was.

Thank You, God, for Gemma.

A farm loomed ahead. A narrow and unpaved service road lay beyond it. That would do just fine.

"Here we go."

He gripped the steering wheel tightly and gunned the engine toward the farm. The truck flew across the field, jolting and bumping across the uneven ground so severely the entire vehicle seemed to shake down to its bolts. They hit the drainage ditch, bounced up on the other side and swerved onto the unpaved road. It wasn't much more than a thin dirt track. The tires spun on the loose soil, threatening to send the truck flying right back off into the ditch again. Then the wheels caught traction. Jackson whispered a prayer of thanksgiving to God and kept driving.

The dirt track gave way to another one, heading southwest. He cut down it, weaving down country roads and any track through the woods he could find. Tree branches scraped against the vehicle. Police chatter filtered through his radio letting him keep track of where Caleb's stolen SUV had last been spotted.

Reese was like a rat in a maze with a dozen talented cats searching for him at once from multiple different angles. It was only a matter of time before someone caught him, Jackson told himself. He just prayed that both Amy and her unborn child would be alive and safe when that happened.

They'd been driving southwest for almost twenty minutes when they crested a narrow bridge over a rural highway surrounded by forest.

"There he is!" Gemma shouted and pointed toward Jackson's window. He glanced to the left just in time to see an RCMP vehicle fly under the bridge and down the highway behind them, with Reese at the wheel and Amy looking petrified but alive in the passenger seat.

"Hold on!" Jackson smashed the brakes and yanked the wheel hard. The truck spun on the narrow bridge. He could hear his sister praying to God that they wouldn't break through the barrier, fly off the overpass and crash down onto the road below. Trees and sky flew past the window. Then finally, with a jarring crash the front of his truck smacked into the barrier fence. They shuttered to a stop.

He leaped out, pulled his weapon, spun toward the departing vehicle and fired, praying his aim would be steady and sure.

Please, Lord, protect Amy and the baby! His bullet caught the back-right tire. It exploded with a bang. The vehicle swerved into a tree and crashed.

He turned to release Hudson from the backseat, but Gemma was already out of the truck and unbuckling his partner. Hudson bounded onto the road.

"Grab the phone!" he told her. The line with the dispatcher remained open.

"On it!" Gemma shouted.

He signaled Hudson to his side, ran to the end of the bridge, jumped a narrow fence and scrambled down an incline to the steep road below. Ahead of him, he could see Reese dragging Amy out of the car and into the woods.

"Stop! Police!" Jackson shouted.

He raised his gun to fire, but he didn't take the shot. He didn't have a clean line of sight and wouldn't risk hurting Amy and Skye.

"We have eyes on the suspect and hostage!" Gemma hurried after him and ran down the road just a few steps behind, yelling into the phone. "Single vehicle collision. We need paramedics and backup."

Jackson and Hudson reached Caleb's smashed-up vehicle. It was empty.

The forest lay dark and quiet ahead of him. He couldn't even see Amy.

"They're sending everyone!" Gemma called. "Police, helicopters, you name it. I gave them both our GPS coordinates and our intersection."

"Well done."

"Thanks." She reached his side and bent over, panting. "But apparently, I don't just need to practice running but also shouting while doing so."

They turned toward the trees. Silence fell. He couldn't see or hear them anywhere. Reese had a head start and was an expert at being silent and staying hidden.

"How do we find them?" Gemma whispered.

"We don't," Jackson said. "But Hudson will."

He looked down at his faithful partner. Hudson was standing at attention, ready for orders.

Gemma's chin rose. "I'm coming with you."

"I have an obligation to order you to remain on the road and stay with the vehicle," he said. "But since I know you won't do that, I'm going to say that however far you think you should hang back, double it. He's got a gun. I just got you back and I don't want to lose my big sister."

His hands clasped hers for a moment. Then he yanked a ski mask from within the vehicle and held it in front of Hudson's nose. The dog sniffed it, then sniffed the ground. His ears perked.

"Search!" Jackson ordered. "Find him! Take him down!"

The dog barked like a general calling them to battle. Then Hudson took off running through the trees, with Jackson on his tail. Jackson was running blind, unable to either see or hear his target, but he trusted in his partner with every step he took.

Hudson's tail was straight, his head was high and his nose sniffed the air as he confidently charged through the trees.

Suddenly a gunshot pierced the forest. Jackson signaled Hudson and stopped. His body froze as

Hudson ran back to his side. Then he glanced through the trees and saw them.

Amy was crouched at the base of a tree. Reese stood over her, with one hand cruelly holding her by the arm. The other hand aimed a gun at her temple. Amy's hands rose and tears streaked her cheeks, but as she glanced at Jackson, he could see the depth of faith and strength shining in her eyes.

"Not another step!" Reese shouted. "Or I will kill her!"

Pain wracked Amy's body. The contractions had started again, stronger, harder and more relentless than they'd been before. Reese gripped her left arm tightly. His violent threats filled her ears. And yet, as she fixed her eyes on Jackson's brave form and the loyal K-9 partner standing by his side, she could feel a fresh strength moving through her.

She was going to survive. She would not let herself die here in these woods.

"Drop your weapon!" Jackson shouted. "Get down on the ground now!"

Hudson barked furiously. The dog's hackles rose.

Reese dug the barrel of the gun painfully into her temple.

"You have no leverage here!" Reese shouted. "Turn around and leave now, or I will shoot her!"

"Take me instead!" Gemma shouted. Suddenly her best friend was running through the trees several feet to the right of Jackson. She stopped, panting, and raised her hands. "I'm the one you want! Not Amy! I'm the one who was looking into the Pine Crest murders. It's my store and home you broke into. I'll give you my laptop and all my research. She doesn't know anything and I'm willing to trade my life for hers!"

Gemma pulled in a deep breath. Then a defiant twinkle shone in her eyes.

"Oh, and surprise, I'm still alive," Gemma shouted. "You didn't actually manage to kill me."

For a moment, Reese didn't move; instead, he looked from Amy, to Jackson, to Gemma, as if they were three different points of the same triangle.

Then Amy felt the barrel of the weapon move away from her head as he turned toward Gemma and set her friend in his sights. And Amy knew she was no longer in the line of fire. She glanced at Jackson. A warning flashed in his eyes as if he could read her mind. But Amy didn't hesitate. She'd always been impulsive. She'd never been one to do what was expected.

And now, Amy hoped, that part of who she was would save everyone's lives.

Her right hand balled into a fist. She spun toward Reese, throwing a punch right into his gut with every ounce of strength she could summon.

He grunted and let go of her arm. She turned to run, only to be sent sprawling forward as Reese grabbed her leg. Amy landed on her hands and knees, then kicked up hard, catching him in the face with a satisfying crack. He dropped his grip again and she scrambled back across the ground, as she heard Jackson shout, "Hudson! Take him down!"

The German shepherd's majestic black-and-tan form leaped over Amy, caught Reese by the shoulder and brought him to the ground. Jackson ran for Reese and wrestled the gun from his grip. He flipped the criminal over and cuffed his hands behind his back.

"Reese Cyan," Jackson said, "I am arresting you for the offense of kidnapping and attempted murder. You have the right to retain and instruct counsel without delay."

Gemma reached Amy's side as Jackson continued to arrest Reese.

"Please tell me you were bluffing to cause a distraction and not actually offering to let him take you," Amy said to her best friend through gritted teeth.

"Sure, let's say that." Gemma crouched down beside her. "Are you okay?"

Amy tried to nod, only a sudden burst of pain

swept over her again. She grabbed her belly as suddenly her eyes met Jackson's. "I think Skye is coming now!"

For a moment, she thought Jackson was about to leave the prisoner on the ground and rush to her side.

Instead, he turned to Gemma. "Stay with her. Tell dispatch we need an airlift to the nearest hospital."

Then his green eyes focused on her face again.

"Amy," he called. "Just keep breathing. It's going to be okay. I promise."

Time blurred through waves of pain, as Jackson hurriedly marched Reese back to Caleb's damaged vehicle, locked him in the back, and then ran back through the woods to join Gemma and Amy. Together, the siblings helped Amy to her feet and slowly walked her through the woods.

Then suddenly she heard the sound of sirens filling the air and the thrum of helicopter rotors overhead.

"Over here!" Jackson shouted. "We need paramedics here now!"

Suddenly law enforcement was rushing through the woods toward them. Paramedics helped Amy onto a stretcher and carried her the rest of the way through the trees, asking her questions about how she was feeling and how far apart her contractions were. Jackson and Gemma flanked her on either side. She looked to her left and saw police taking Reese into custody. Then wind whipped the air around her as a bright orange air ambulance helicopter landed a few yards to their right.

A flight paramedic in a fluorescent yellow jacket ran toward them. He glanced at the siblings. "Which one of you is coming with her?"

Amy glanced at Jackson. His deep and fathomless eyes met hers.

I want it to be you. I don't know why, but I want you by my side.

But he broke her gaze and looked at his sister.

"You should go with Amy," he said. "I'll wrap things up here."

Amy felt herself whisked onto the helicopter. Paramedics were checking her vitals. An oxygen mask was placed over her face to help slow her breathing.

She looked back to see Jackson and Hudson standing alone on the road.

Then the helicopter door closed, blocking Jackson from her view, and she felt the air ambulance begin to rise.

THIRTEEN

Jackson paced circles around the Huntsville hospital waiting room. It had been over four hours since Amy had been airlifted from the forest just outside South River and two and a half hours since Jackson and Hudson had arrived there in his truck. Thankfully, despite a dented front bumper, it still drove just fine. According to his sister, Amy had been rushed into surgery as soon as she'd arrived. Since then, there had been nothing to do but wait, pace and pray.

Now Gemma sat curled up on a plastic chair furiously typing something into her phone, and Hudson lay spread out under her seat. The German shepherd's eyes followed Jackson's path around the room.

Gemma sighed and ran one hand through her hair, so that it stuck up between her fingers.

"What are you doing?" Jackson asked.

"I'm trying to find a missing person's report that matches our Jane Doe," Gemma said.

She frowned at the screen.

Jackson sat down beside her. "What Jane Doe?"

Gemma glanced up at him. "You told me that a female body was found washed up downriver from where my car crashed."

"Yes," he said. "But the only reason Finnick alerted me to that is because local police thought it was you."

"I know," Gemma said. "But just because she wasn't me, and isn't related to the Pine Crest case, doesn't mean she isn't somebody. She was a person with a life that's now over. Someone loved her and is wondering where she is."

She fixed her bright green eyes on her brother's face.

"Now, we know police think the body was female," Gemma said. "She was found in the river, she didn't have any identifying belongings on her and police didn't ask you to do a visual identification but were relying on DNA. That means that either she was dead so long that she had significantly decomposed, which doesn't seem probable considering they thought it was me—"

"Or that she was a victim of the kind of severe attack that doesn't leave belongings and makes the victim hard to identify," Jackson finished.

"Right," Gemma said, "so it's unlikely to be an accidental death. It's more probable that someone killed her and then tried to destroy the body and any trace of who she was."

Jackson leaned over and kissed his sister on the top of her head.

"I like who you are and how your mind works," he said.

She laughed. "So, you'll help me make sure that she doesn't become a cold case?"

"Absolutely."

It definitely beat pacing. Jackson and Gemma sat side by side, typing on their phones and searching various missing person's reports. Eventually, after about an hour they identified a young woman who had gone missing a few weeks prior. Police had dismissed it as a runaway. Her family had been convinced her ex-boyfriend murdered her.

"I'll flag this to all the right people," Jackson said. "Hopefully they have her DNA on file and can check Jane Doe against it. It may not be good news for the family."

"But it will be closure," Gemma said.

A tired-looking male nurse with a trim beard and pale blue scrubs appeared in the doorway.

"I'm looking for the friends and family of Amy Scout," he called.

Jackson leaped to his feet. So did Gemma, and Hudson wriggled out from under the seat to join them.

"That's us," Jackson said.

Gemma squeezed her brother's arm and he patted her hand reassuringly.

"I'm happy to tell you that Skye Elizabeth Scout was born at 2:15 a.m.," he said. The nurse's smile was tired but genuine. "She weighed in at five pounds, six ounces. Both mother and baby are doing fine and recovering well."

"Oh, thank You, God." Jackson breathed a prayer.

For a moment he felt his knees threaten to buckle out from under him. But then his sister grabbed him and hugged him tightly.

"They're okay," Gemma said, tears choking her voice. "Amy and the baby are okay."

Relief and joy cascaded through Jackson's heart like thunderous waves.

"They're being moved into a recovery room now," the nurse went on. "They will be free to see visitors soon."

Gemma and Jackson released each other and turned back toward the nurse.

"Thank you," Jackson said.

"I take it you're the father?" the nurse asked Jackson. "You're welcome to come see her and meet your baby now."

Jackson felt his mouth go dry.

"No," he said. "Thank you, but I'm not the father. I'm… I'm her best friend's brother."

"Oh, I'm sorry," the nurse said. He blinked.

"I thought Mrs. Scout's husband was here to see the baby."

The nurse nodded and disappeared back down the hallway.

"I seriously doubt Paul has somehow rushed to small-town Canada to check in on Amy," Gemma said, dryly. "I can assume Amy told you what a nasty piece of work he is?"

"Yeah," Jackson said. He dropped back into his chair, suddenly feeling deflated. Hudson lay down on his feet. Something about the nurse's well-meaning and maybe predictable misunderstanding had left him spent.

Who was Jackson to Amy? What was Amy to him?

Were they even friends? Or just acquaintances?

He wasn't her boyfriend, her husband or the father of her child. Not someone who had stepped up and promised to be there for her and have a role in her future.

Despite the fact he wanted to be everything to her, he was nothing to her at all.

"What would you say to popping outside and getting some fresh air?" his sister said, cutting through his thoughts.

"Yeah," he answered and stood up again. That wasn't a bad idea and maybe it would help him clear his mind. "I'm sure Hudson would really appreciate getting a walk."

The dog's tail thumped in agreement. He clipped Hudson's leash onto his harness and the three of them headed out of the maternity ward, down the hall and into the main lobby. Suddenly, Hudson woofed happily and his tail started wagging. A moment later Jackson saw why. A tall man with silver-gray hair, wearing blue jeans and a blazer, was standing by the front desk, with a black Labrador retriever sitting at his feet. Jackson blinked.

"Inspector Finnick!" he exclaimed. "What are you doing here?"

Jackson rushed over to his boss as Finnick turned, stepped away from the desk and smiled. Hudson and the black Lab wagged their tails and nuzzled each other in greeting.

"Gemma," Jackson said. "I'd like to introduce you to my boss, Inspector Ethan Finnick, head of the RCMP's Ontario K-9 Unit and his K-9 partner, Nippy."

"Short for Nipissing," Finnick said, with a smile. "All of the dogs in our unit are named after major Ontario lakes and rivers."

"This is my sister," Jackson added. "Gemma Locke."

"It's very nice to meet you," Finnick said, smiling at Gemma. "I'm glad to see you're alive and well."

"Nice to meet you too," Gemma said. She

shook his hand. "Thank you for giving my brother time to come up here and look for me."

"What are you doing here?" Jackson asked.

"I'd driven up to the area to check in on Caleb," Finnick said. "He's doing great, by the way. He's got a few stitches and an impressive-looking scar, but nothing serious to worry about. He'll be released tomorrow. Since I was driving all the way up to South River, I figured I'd also swing by here on the way back for an update."

"Did you hear Amy had the baby?" Jackson asked. "Five pounds something. Baby and mother are both doing well."

Finnick's smile widened. "That's really awesome to hear."

"We were just about to go for a walk," Jackson said. "Do you want to join us?"

"Absolutely," Finnick said.

The five of them stepped through the automatic doors and out into the parking lot. The sky was inky black and dotted with hundreds more stars than Jackson would ever see back in the city. He stepped back and turned to his sister.

"Gemma's been busy trying to identify the Jane Doe that was mistaken for her and thinks it could be a young missing woman who was identified as a runaway," Jackson told Finnick, as they made their way through the parking lot. "Those seniors at Pine Crest really opened my eyes to how frustrating it is when cops don't solve a case and get justice for your loved ones."

True, he'd known intellectually that Gemma had been frustrated with how police had handled the disappearance of her friend Louise. But being confronted head-on by the seniors had hit him with that reality in a new and deeper way.

Or maybe something inside himself had changed.

"Well, loop me in on what you've got and I'll see what I can do," Finnick said.

They followed a path down the side of the hospital. Slowly the noise of vehicles and people coming in and out of the parking lot faded, until they were completely alone. Finnick glanced around as if ensuring no one would be able to overhear them.

"So, as you know, Reese Cyan has been arrested," Finnick said. "He's being charged with kidnapping and attempted murder. He will be arraigned in the morning. We're already hearing reports from jurisdictions across the country where he's wanted on charges of both theft and trafficking in stolen property. Thankfully pawnshops are required to keep meticulous records and it now appears some pieces of jewelry he pawned in Toronto over a decade ago matched some of the items stolen from the Pine Crest Retirement Home. I'll make sure we test his DNA against the DNA collected from the Pine Crest scene. I'll also suggest opening an internal investigation into what went wrong with the initial investigation of these murders."

"Do you think there was corruption or some kind of police criminality involved?" Gemma asked.

"No," Finnick said. "Just really sloppy police work. More should've been done at the time to check to see if anything had been pawned and that DNA should've been tested years ago. No promises that we'll be able to pin the murders on Reese too, but we'll be investigating."

"I can't believe we're so close to giving those people at Pine Crest closure," Gemma said, "and yet we're still not quite there."

"Don't worry," Finnick said. "We're not about to give up just because it's hard."

"You'd be hard-pressed to find anybody who cares about solving cold cases more than Finnick here," Jackson said.

Finnick chuckled wryly. "Yeah, I've been fighting for us to get our own dedicated cold case unit for a long time."

A narrow park lay to their right with trees and benches. Streetlamps flickered on overhead as they approached, sending gentle pools of light down at their feet.

Jackson let Gemma and Finnick walk on ahead

while he fell into step behind them. They let their K-9 partners off their leashes. Hudson and Nippy ran around the park, charging at each other, rolling in the grass, but never straying too far from their humans.

"Your brother sent me pictures of your office wall," Finnick said with what sounded like genuine admiration. "I have to say I'm impressed. Your investigative work on half a dozen of those cases is absolutely incredible. I think it's a shame that you're not pursuing a career in police work."

"Thanks, but I don't," Gemma said, and Jackson could hear the smile in her voice. "Some people don't like talking to cops, sometimes for good reasons and other times for stupid reasons. A private investigator can get leads that police can't. Also, there are procedures in place that impact what cases you go after, and private investigators don't have those limitations."

"All true," Finnick said, "but we have a lot more resources. Which is why we need a dedicated unit."

"That works in cooperation with civilian investigators?" Gemma asked.

Finnick chuckled then glanced back at Jackson. "I can see why you told me your sister is relentless and tenacious."

Jackson listened a moment longer as Gemma and Finnick talked back and forth about various cold cases Gemma had been investigating and their theories on each. Jackson was almost jealous. He'd never felt like he was completely on the same wavelength as either his sister or his boss—as much as he genuinely admired both—and yet they were clearly cut from the same cloth.

"You and Caleb created a bit of a stir when you visited Pine Crest," Finnick told Jackson. "Several of the seniors posted on social media." He glanced over to where Hudson was play-fighting with Nippy. "Apparently, although they had mixed feelings on what the police were doing about the case, they all thought Hudson was absolutely adorable and should star in his own series of crime movies."

Jackson laughed. "Yeah, well, I'm glad I got to meet them," he said. "When all this blows over, I'm happy to help push for this unit you want to set up to anyone who'll listen."

A sudden wave of pride filled his core.

"Also, I hope you and my sister stay in touch," Jackson added. "Because if you want members of the public pushing for this, there is no better person in your corner than Gemma. She genuinely cares about the little guy and will be relentless in doing what it takes to help them."

Gemma laughed. "Thank you, bro."

"You're welcome," he said, "and while I'm

sorry I wasn't there for you earlier, sis, I'm completely behind you now."

"I have to ask you something..." Finnick glanced at Gemma. "What was it about the Pine Crest case that got your attention? Why that case?"

Gemma ran both hands through her hair and laughed. "I had a theory," she said, "which I now realize is ridiculous, now that we know about Reese Cyan."

"And what was that?" Finnick asked.

"I thought Kenny Stanton might possibly be Amy's ex-husband, Paul Keebles."

She laughed, but Jackson didn't. He felt his whole body stiffen.

"What do you mean you thought Amy's ex-husband could be the Pine Crest killer?" Jackson asked, so sharply that Gemma stopped walking suddenly and turned back to face him. So did Finnick. He noticed his boss wasn't smiling and hadn't seemed to find the thought funny either.

"Okay," Gemma said, "so it turned out Paul had a lot of pseudonyms, including Paul Kent and Stanley Paul. And I thought if you put Ken and Stan together..."

"You get Kenny Stanton," Jackson said. "I get the link, but it's weak."

"I know," Gemma said and shrugged. "And after Reese tried to murder me, I realized I wasn't dealing with some two-bit conman after all but someone much more dangerous. The idea that Paul could be Kenny just got stuck in my mind and I couldn't shake it, especially after Amy told me Paul loved showing off these medals that his grandfather supposedly won in the Second World War. Which got me thinking, what if Paul had once lived in Canada? What if while he'd been here, he worked at a seniors' residence and messed around with some senior citizens' pain IVs when he was younger and accidentally killed them?"

"It's very tenuous," Jackson said, slowly. "But not impossible. After all, Reese Cyan only has a record of theft and trafficking in stolen property, and we had no problem jumping to the conclusion that he was capable of murder."

"Right," Gemma said. "But I couldn't find any evidence that Paul had ever even been up here."

Just like they hadn't thought it was possible that he was up here now.

Suddenly a thought washed over him, jolting his system like freezing-cold water.

He summoned Hudson, turned and started running back to the front door.

"Where are you going?" Gemma called.

"The nurse told us he thought Skye's father was here in the hospital!" Jackson shouted. "We assumed it was a misunderstanding. What if it's not? What if Paul was working with Reese Cyan and thinks Amy has unknowingly seen evidence that could put him away for three murders?"

Amy lay in her hospital bed and looked over at the tiny bundle lying in the cot beside her. Her eyes traced her daughter's sleeping form. Skye's tiny fingers were curled into fists. Her eyes were closed and her little button nose was scrunched in sleep.

A joy deeper than any happiness Amy had ever known welled up inside her.

"You're perfect," she whispered to her tiny child. "You're safe, you're here and you're so very, very loved. I will do everything in my power to take care of you."

"Knock-knock," a female voice called from the doorway. Amy looked up to see an elderly nurse pop her head around the corner.

"I was wondering if you were up for visitors?" the nurse said. "I've got somebody special here who's been dying to meet the little one."

Jackson.

Amy smiled. "Yes, please send him in."

A giant bouquet of red roses came through the door along with the largest teddy bear Amy had ever seen, completely blocking the face and body of the person carrying them.

"I'm so sorry I didn't make it here sooner,

darling, but I had a nightmare of a time getting here." The voice was male but definitely not Jackson's. "Why did you choose to have our child somewhere so many hours' drive away from an airport?"

Her fingers grabbed ahold of the blanket and held it tightly.

No, no, it can't be...

Through a haze of painkillers and exhaustion, she watched as Paul set the abundance of flowers and the teddy bear down on a table. He looked older than she remembered. Something about his expensive-looking suit and tie made her think of somebody wearing a "rich man" costume in a low-budget play. The lines on his face seemed deeper too, making the huge, broad grin that he flashed seem more like a grimace.

He thanked the nurse, closed the door and pulled the curtains shut.

"There," Paul said. "That's better. Now we're alone."

"How...how did you find me?" Her words felt slow and sluggish. "How did you know I was here?"

Paul chortled. He walked toward her, barely even glancing at the tiny baby in the cot on the other side of her bed.

"Don't start thinking silly thoughts," he said. "Of course I was going to know where you are.

I have a whole team of lawyers for things like that. I've got people up here keeping an eye on you, and when you checked in to the hospital, they called and alerted me that my wife was having my child."

He had people up in Northern Ontario? And were these the same "lawyers" that had told Gemma he was getting a restraining order against both of them? No, he had to be lying. What he was saying wasn't making sense.

"I don't believe you," Amy said. "That's not a thing that lawyers do, and hospitals don't give out information like that."

"You're just confused because you're tired." He leaned over and patted her hand, pressing it firmly into the mattress. Then he picked up the emergency call button the nurse had left her with and moved it onto the dresser behind him. "Trust me, sweetie, you're not thinking straight. Your horrible friend Gemma tried to poison your mind with all sorts of ridiculous lies about me. And now you're just so tired and confused that you don't know your up from your down."

His voice was soothing, sweet and gentle. Paul had always been charming, and everybody had always loved him. But his million-watt grin didn't work on her anymore. Paul had fooled her once and wouldn't trick her again.

Charming guy...everybody loved him...

The words started kicking insistently at the back of her mind, like they were trying to get her attention. Where had she heard them recently?

She pulled her hand away from his, dug both palms into the hospital bed and pushed herself up to sitting.

"Everything you told me was a lie," Amy said. Her voice sounded weak to her own ears, and yet she felt it growing stronger with every word. "You have other wives and other kids. You had multiple fake names and identities! You broke my heart and you shattered my trust, and I don't want anything to do with you now. I want you to get out of my room. I don't know who you really are and I don't care. Our relationship was a lie, our marriage was a fake and I'm going to do everything in my power to keep you out of Skye's life. So go ahead and call your team of imaginary lawyers on me. I'm never going to let you hurt me again."

Paul stepped back as if she'd slapped him. His face paled. "Honey, you're being silly and you're getting emotional."

"You're right I'm emotional!" Amy said. "I have every right to be. In fact, my heart is absolutely full to the brim with deeper emotions than a shallow conman like you could ever dream of. Like determination and pride. I'm feeling gratitude for my friends, and I'm feeling love for my child. When you met me I didn't know who I was or where I was going. You took advantage of that. Now I know who I am and what I'm capable of."

Paul leaned over her. His face loomed just inches above hers.

"Keep your voice down, sweetie," he hissed.

"Or you'll do what?" Amy said. "I'm not impressed by you anymore, and you definitely don't scare me. You have any idea how strong I am? Or how much courage it took for me to go through what I lived through in the past few months or the last couple of days? I'm stronger than you could ever possibly imagine. You might say you come from a long line of military veterans and your grandfather might've served in the Air Force—or whatever other lies you tell to make yourself seem big—but you're so weak all you can do is try to make yourself feel big by waving around somebody else's medals and memorabilia…"

Her words trailed off as she suddenly realized what she'd said.

Paul had shown her the Second World War Air Force medals and memorabilia…

Like the ones stolen from the Pine Crest victim…

By the charming man everyone had loved, but who'd disappeared…

In a case Gemma had been looking into without telling her but had been so invested in, she'd nearly died to chase a lead.

Amy felt her face pale and the truth began to dawn.

"What military did your grandfather serve in again?" she asked.

Paul snorted. "Good old U. S. of A., of course."

Right, she knew Paul was American. But she remembered the medals he'd shown her had a crown in the insignia. She thought of Blake's story about her AWOL husband. The American military's insignia didn't have a crown on it. But Canada's did.

"And how did you know I was here and then get here so quickly?" she pressed. "It would take hours to get here from the States."

He chuckled again, and it sounded even more forced. "I told you, I've got people up here."

"But what people?" she asked. "Where are they? And who did you have keeping tabs on me? And why me? I can't imagine you have people keeping tabs on all the women you've hurt and abandoned."

He didn't answer right away. She had no doubt his mind was swirling for an answer. But her mind was working faster. Too many things weren't adding up. She'd thought she'd seen Reese Cyan somewhere before. What if Reese had been the business contact Paul kept flying up to Canada to see…? What if he was the fence who Paul had used to sell the stuff he stole from the various people he conned? That would explain how Paul knew where she was living and what hospital she'd gone to. Maybe he'd been using Reese to keep tabs on her for weeks.

Amy had told Jackson that Paul never cared about her enough to try to hurt her. But it would be a whole lot different if Paul thought her friend Gemma could prove that he'd committed murder.

"You're Kenny Stanton." Her voice barely rose above a whisper. "Aren't you?"

She half expected him to laugh and deny it. Like he'd lied to her face so many times before. But instead, for the first time since she'd met him, fear filled Paul's face. He recoiled.

"That's… I'm… It's not… How do you know that name?"

He stammered as his usually golden tongue struggled for words. Amy's gaze darted from the tiny child in the cot beside her to the emergency button he'd placed behind him.

What would Paul do if she reached for the call button? What would happen if she shouted for help? Would anyone even hear her over the hustle and bustle of the maternity ward?

Lord, I need Your help now. Protect me and my child.

"Help!" Amy yelled as loudly as she could. "I need security in here now!"

Suddenly, Paul's face went red. The mask of civility fell from his eyes. He lunged at her. With one hand, he grabbed her by the throat and pinned her down against the bed. She pushed him back as hard as she could.

But she was still weak from giving birth, and he had the upper hand.

Paul clamped his fingers around her throat and squeezed, blocking the air from her lungs. With the other he pushed the button on her IV to increase the amount of medication swamping her system.

"Now, I told you not to get any silly ideas in your head," he whispered. "You're not thinking straight. Once we get out of here and go somewhere quiet, I'll explain everything. You will listen and then I'll fix this mess and everything will be okay."

No.

But she could feel herself getting weaker. Blackness was seeping into the corners of her eyes. Any moment now she was going to pass out. She was at the mercy of a killer. One who wouldn't hesitate to snuff out her life.

Help me, Lord! Save my child!

Darkness swept in and the world went black.

FOURTEEN

"Where is Amy Scout's room?" Jackson stood at the reception desk and showed his badge to the same male nurse he'd spoken to before. "I need someone to take us there, immediately. I have reason to believe she could be in danger."

"This way, officer." The nurse leapt to his feet immediately and gestured to a woman in scrubs to come take over his post.

The nurse led Jackson quickly down a maze of hallways. Jackson had Hudson by his side, and Finnick, Nippy and Gemma followed close behind. He'd rarely been so well reinforced, and yet he'd never felt more lost and terrified.

He had to be wrong. Amy and Skye had to be okay…

Lord, I need them to be safe, like I need the air that I breathe.

Jackson heard the plaintive sound of a tiny baby wailing. His chest ached and somehow he knew that it was Skye.

The nurse's footsteps quickened. Jackson's heart pounded so hard he could feel it in his chest. The nurse reached a closed door, knocked twice and then opened it. "Excuse me, ma'am, but you've got the police here to see you."

The words froze on the nurse's tongue and a second later Jackson saw why. The bed was empty. Amy was gone. Skye was alone in her crib. Instantly, Gemma slipped past them into the room and swept Skye up into her arms, comforting her and holding her to her chest.

Jackson turned to the nurse. "Where is Amy?"

"I don't know," the nurse said, gravely. "But I will find out."

The nurse ran to the nearest internal phone and called in a missing patient report. Jackson could only hear his side of the conversation, but it was clear the hospital would be going into lockdown until she could be found.

Jackson prayed it wasn't too late. Hudson whimpered and pressed his snout into Jackson's hand. Skye had begun to settle down in Gemma's arms.

His sister's large, worried eyes met his. "What's happening?"

"I don't know," Jackson said.

He stood by Gemma and Skye, as Finnick ran down the hallway, stopping person after person, flashing his badge and asking if anyone knew where the patient in room 812 had gone. The nurse ended his call and turned toward Jackson. His face was so pale it was almost gray.

"Apparently, someone spotted her leaving the maternity ward a few moments ago," he said. "She was in a wheelchair and being pushed by a balding man who identified himself as her husband and said he was taking her for fresh air."

"He's not her husband!" Jackson shouted. A cold, near paralyzing fear filled his gut. "He's a suspect in a triple homicide."

"I'll get to the security office and coordinate the response," Finnick called. "Jackson, go find Amy."

"I've got Skye!" Gemma added. "I'll keep her safe. You go!"

Jackson silently thanked God for them, then he looked down at his partner. The dog was standing at attention. Jackson looped the dog's leash tightly around his hand.

"Hudson," he ordered, "find Amy!"

His partner barked and then took off running down the hospital hallways, dragging Jackson behind them. They pushed past startled staff and visitors, running as fast as Jackson's legs would allow, even as he could feel his partner pulling him to go even faster. Hudson led him through a maze of back corridors and service hallways, into the quieter and more isolated areas of the hospital. They ran through a large laundry room and the sound of sheets and towels rolling and tumbling rose around them.

An emergency exit loomed ahead. Hudson's barks echoed around them as the dog practically threw himself at the door. Jackson pushed it open and they burst through into an alley behind the hospital. It was empty. Hudson's snout rose. He sniffed the air. Then he barked again, turned and led Jackson down to the end of the alley. An even narrower laneway lay ahead. They turned into it. There was an empty wheelchair lying on its side. One wheel still spun in the air.

Then Jackson saw them. Paul was trying to drag a semiconscious Amy into the back of a white delivery van, while she fought and struggled against him.

Jackson turned to his partner and unclipped Hudson's leash.

"Go get him!" he called. "Take him down! Save Amy!"

Hudson charged toward Paul, with Jackson running a few steps behind. Startled, the criminal dropped Amy onto the ground, where she crumpled like a rag doll, and took off running. In a moment, Jackson had reached her, lifted her up and cradled her into his arms.

"Jackson?" Her voice was weak. Amy's head fell against his shoulder. "Is that really you?"

"Yeah, it's really me," he whispered. "It's okay. I've got you, and Gemma's got Skye. You're safe."

Paul sprinted down the alley, but he was no match for Hudson's strength and speed. With a triumphant howl, Hudson launched himself at Paul. His strong paws hit him in the back and knocked him to the pavement, pinning him there. A door clanged open behind them. Jackson looked back to see uniformed security officers and police spilling out into the alleyway.

"You found her?" a man in a dark blue uniform shouted at Jackson.

"Yup, she's safe!" Jackson called. "I've got her."

Officers ran past him. Jackson ordered Hudson to release Paul as the officers stepped in to arrest him. Hudson returned to Jackson's side, leaned his paws against Jackson's leg and licked Amy's fingers. She ran her hand over the dog's head.

"It's all over," Jackson said. "Paul's being taken into custody right now. Hudson took him down."

Amy smiled. Her eyes fluttered open and then closed again. "Good dog."

"Very good dog," he said.

But it seemed he'd spoken too soon as a flurry of shouting and activity rose from the end of the alley behind him. He turned. Somehow Paul had managed to wriggle free from his arresting officer. Paul had taken off running again down another alley in the direction of the parking lot, with a half dozen people on his trail shouting at him to stop.

"They underestimated him," Amy said weakly. "Like I did."

"Don't worry," Jackson said. "He won't get away this time."

A gunshot sounded somewhere out of view. More shouts rose and Amy pushed herself closer into Jackson's chest. Hudson growled toward the departing group and glanced up at Jackson. He could read the question in his partner's eyes.

"No, buddy," Jackson told Hudson, and his voice sounded gruff to his ears. "Not this time. We're going to let somebody else deal with bringing the bad guy to justice right now. Our job is protecting Amy."

He turned and walked back toward the open hospital door, with Amy in his arms and Hudson by his side. As he stepped through the doorway, a nurse offered to take Amy, but Jackson shook his head. "It's okay, I've got her."

Jackson carried Amy in his arms all the way back to her hospital room where Gemma waited, still holding the sleeping infant. A soft cry escaped Amy's beautiful lips as her eyes alighted on her baby girl.

"Skye's safe," Gemma said. Happy tears filled her eyes. Hudson's ears perked as he sniffed in the direction of the tiny, sleeping child as if mem-orizing her scent. Gemma laid the baby back to rest in her cot. "She's perfect, Amy."

Gently and tenderly, Jackson set Amy down on the bed.

"It's all going to be okay now," he whispered. He eased his arms out from under her. "I won't let anything happen to you or Skye, I promise."

A fleet of medical staff in uniform filled the doorway. Gemma slipped past them and out of the room. Jackson turned to follow.

But Amy grabbed his hand. "Stay with me. Please."

He swallowed hard.

"I'm going to have to give the doctors and nurses some space to do their thing," he said. "But I'll be right outside the door and I'll come back in as soon as they give me permission. Okay?"

Amy nodded weakly. "Okay."

He signaled Hudson to his side. They stepped out of Amy's room. The nurse they'd spoken to before nodded to Jackson and closed the door behind them.

Gemma was standing a few feet away in the hallway.

"You okay?" Gemma asked. "You look ex-hausted. You want to go grab a quick bite or even just a drink of water?"

"No, I'm staying," Jackson said. He wasn't surprised he looked tired, and he was sure fatigue would hit him like a ton of bricks later. But for now, he stood up straight and crossed his arms. Hudson sat at attention by his side. "Amy asked me to stay and I promised her I wouldn't leave."

His sister's green eyes searched his face for a long moment, as if Gemma was seeing him for the first time. Finally she nodded.

"Well, I'm going to go get a drink of water for you and one for Hudson too," she said. Gemma turned as if to go, then she hesitated, turned back and gave him a hug. "I'm really proud of you, brother."

He opened his mouth to thank her, only to find a lump in his throat so large he couldn't get the words out. Instead, he nodded to his sister, she nodded back, then Gemma turned and started down the hallway.

Time ticked by slowly, punctuated only by the round clock on the wall and his own worried thoughts. After a few minutes, Finnick and Nippy appeared around the corner and started down the hallway toward them.

"I hear you've got our girl safe and sound," Finnick said, but Jackson couldn't help but notice he was frowning. "Well done."

Jackson felt his spine straighten even further.

"Yes, sir," he said. "Doctors are just checking her over now."

"That's good," Finnick said. The frown lines in his forehead grew even deeper. "It looks like we've lost our main suspect."

Jackson blinked. "Paul got away?"

"No, he's dead." Finnick ran his hand over the back of his head. "It was a stupid, senseless death. He ran into the parking lot, with cops barely three feet behind him, tried to pull a gun on a motorist and hijack her vehicle. She grabbed the gun in self-defense, they fought for it and it went off. They tried to rush him into surgery, but it was too late. He's gone."

Jackson sucked in a breath. "How's the woman?"

"In shock," Finnick said. "But thankfully she's fine." He shook his head. "This whole situation is so infuriating. If he is the man behind the Pine Crest murders, and investigators had done their job in the first place, so much pain and suffering could've been avoided."

The hospital door opened behind him, and medical staff filed out again. A nurse informed Jackson that Amy was ready for him to come back in. She was groggy and would probably sleep for a while, due to the large dose of meds that Paul had hit her with, but that thankfully she'd be okay.

Jackson thanked him, and Finnick excused

himself. Then Jackson took Hudson back into Amy's room, closing the door behind them. She was sitting up in bed. The pink had already begun to return to her cheeks and her face was a little less pale than it had been when he'd left her. But her eyes widened as she clocked his expression.

"What happened?" she asked. "Is everything okay?"

"Am I that transparent?" Jackson asked.

"To me you are."

He crossed the room and crouched down beside her bed.

"I don't know how to tell you this," he said. "But Paul has died."

A sob choked in her throat as he filled Amy in on everything that Finnick had told him. He reached for her and hugged her tightly as she buried her face in his shoulder for a long moment. When she pulled back and he let her go, he noticed that while tears filled her beautiful eyes, they'd stopped before they could even fall.

"Such a waste of a life," she said, bitterly. "He was so talented, smart and charming. But he used those talents to lie, cheat, steal, con, swindle and even kill. Up until the very last moments of his life, he was trying to take advantage of some poor woman." She closed her eyes and prayed. "Thank You, God, that he's finally been stopped."

"Amen."

They talked about the case for a few more minutes, but soon Amy's eyelids fluttered and then closed. So, Jackson settled himself down in a chair opposite the bed, with Hudson by his feet. And that's where he stayed for the next few hours, as Amy slept. Gemma came back with water and some snacks for him and Hudson. She sat with them in silence for a while, and then after an hour told him she was going to get hotel rooms for them both in the area in case Amy and Skye needed to stay a few days. Finnick popped back in too, to let Jackson know he was heading back to the city. Medical staff came in and out to check vitals on the machine by Amy's bed. Skye woke briefly and fussed but settled back into sleep when Jackson scooped the tiny baby into his arms and rocked her gently.

Still Amy slept and Jackson stayed. He wasn't about to leave her side or risk her waking up to find he'd left her.

He was going to be there for Amy as long as she needed him. And then when Amy no longer needed him and could stand on her own two feet again, then what? He didn't know. All he knew was that what had started as a youthful crush so many years ago had grown into something so much deeper and stronger than he ever could've possibly imagined.

He loved Amy Scout and her newborn baby.

He wanted to be there for them always, take care of them and keep them safe, in whatever way Amy wanted, for the rest of their lives.

He hadn't even realized he'd dozed off while sitting in the uncomfortable chair until he heard Amy calling his name and looked up to see the rising sun filtering through the windows.

"Jackson?" She whispered his name like music.

He looked over. She was sitting up in bed, with Skye tucked peacefully in the crook of her arm fast asleep.

He swallowed hard, as an unfamiliar lump formed in his throat.

"I'm here," he said, softly. He walked over and knelt beside the bed. "How are you feeling?"

"I'm good." Her free hand reached for his. He looped his fingers through hers. She held his hand tightly.

"She's amazing, isn't she?" Amy whispered.

Love filled her hazel eyes as she looked down at the baby in her arms. Something fierce and protective moved through his core.

"She's incredible," he said.

He looked from the tiny sleeping child to Amy's radiant face and knew that he'd never seen anything more beautiful in his life.

"*You're* incredible, Amy," Jackson said softly. "You're brilliant, brave and incredibly strong. I meant every word I said yesterday about being there for you and Skye. Whatever you need and whatever comes next, you can count on me. I promise, because—"

I love you, Amy.

The words crossed his heart, but before he could speak them, Amy pulled her hand from his and pressed her fingers against his lips.

"Don't say it," she said. "I know what you're going to say. And I feel it too. You're the most incredible man I've ever met. You're amazing and kind. You apologize for your mistakes and you're committed to growth... But we can't say those words to each other. Not yet. Not now."

He nodded to tell her he understood. She took his hand again.

"All my life I've been impulsive," she said. "I've rushed headlong into things without considering the consequences. And you deserve better than that. We both do. So I can't let myself rush into this. Not until I know for certain that I'm ready."

Jackson swallowed hard.

But what if she was never ready? What if the time never came?

Lord, please give me the strength I need to wait for her and be patient.

"Okay," he said.

"Thank you."

Amy leaned toward him, he bent down toward

her, and their lips met in a kiss that was sweet
and tender. Yet somehow it also felt as if they
were both glancing through an open door before
closing it again.

Then Amy leaned back against the pillow and
fell asleep, holding his hand.

FIFTEEN

The early November air was crisp with the promise of winter, as Amy stepped through the sliding doors of the South River Medical Center following Skye's checkup. She moved across the parking lot, with a diaper bag slung over her shoulder and her daughter nestled safely on her hip. On the other side of the road, she could see forest stretched out to the horizon in a maze of orange, red and gold leaves.

She scanned the lot. Where was Gemma?

"Anybody need a taxi?" Jackson's warm voice rang out from among the parked cars.

A moment later she saw him striding toward her. A lopsided grin crossed his handsome face. Joy shone in his eyes. Amy felt her heart skip a beat. Skye squealed and waved her chubby arms in greeting.

"What are you doing here?" She rushed toward him. "I thought Gemma was coming to get me."

"She had to rush back to the cottage for an unexpected thing," he said. "And I had an errand up here anyway, so it all worked out. I hope this is an okay surprise. Gemma said there was no cell phone reception inside the clinic."

"It's a great surprise."

He opened his arms for her, and she stepped into the warmth of his chest. She felt his beard brush against her cheek.

Jackson had become like a part of the family in the months since Skye had been born. He'd taken a two-week vacation from work immediately after her birth to help Amy, Gemma and the baby get settled in the cottage. And then he'd come up to visit almost every weekend since, to bring groceries, help with Skye, cook, clean, babysit and rebuild his friendship with his sister. Not to mention the countless hours Amy and Jackson had spent together walking, talking, reading, boating, doing the dishes or just being together in comfortable silence.

They pulled apart again.

"What kind of errand and what kind of thing?" she asked.

"My errand is at Pine Crest," he said, "and I'll let Gemma tell you her own thing back at the cottage. It's nothing bad, I promise."

"Okay." She smiled and said, "I trust you."

And she did. He stretched out his hand for the diaper bag and she let him take it. Then he reached for Skye, and the little girl practically launched herself into his arms.

Jackson chuckled and wrapped his arms around Skye, and she reached up and patted his face.

"Hello, princess," he said. Then he glanced at Amy. "How did her checkup go? It's her six-month one, right?"

"Yup," she said. They walked through the parking lot toward his vehicle. "Just routine."

"And how is she?" Jackson's eyes were still on Skye.

"Absolutely perfect."

"Ha! I could've told you that."

As they reached Jackson's truck, she could see Hudson's head sticking out the front window. But as they approached, Hudson leaped into the backseat and curled up beside Skye's car seat. Jackson opened the back door and buckled her in.

"Goggy!" Sky shouted as she flopped her head sideways onto Hudson with a giggle. He licked her cheek.

"Yes, sweetie," Amy said. "Hudson is a big fluffy doggy."

Jackson's eyebrows rose. "Is that her first word?"

"Doggy?" Amy translated, with a laugh. "It might be. Are you jealous?"

"Of Hudson?" Jackson asked. "Always. He's everybody's favorite."

"Not mine," she said.

His eyes met hers and held them for a long moment. Then he opened her door for her. Once she was inside, he walked around to his side, stepped in, and they started driving.

"Do you have an update on the investigation?" she asked.

"Not this time," Jackson said. "I just need to drop something off quickly to a friend."

Jackson and Hudson had made several visits to Pine Crest Retirement Home in the past few months to fill them in on the case as it developed, sometimes with Gemma, Amy and Skye in tow. After Paul's death, his DNA had come back as a match to Kenny Stanton's. Several seniors had also made a positive photo identification, and military medals found in Paul's home had turned out to belong to murdered veteran Gordon Donnelly.

While Paul died before he saw justice, Amy knew it had given the residents a degree of peace to know the case had finally been solved. Thanks to some firm pushing from Finnick, an investigation had been opened into how the original case had been bungled too, with several current and retired officers being brought in for questioning. Thankfully, Reese had pled guilty to the kidnapping and working with Paul to fence stolen items, saving Amy the ordeal of having to testify against him at trial. Investigators across Canada and the United States were still unraveling the mystery of the man who'd called himself Paul Keebles, his multiple aliases, and the many people he'd lied to and stolen from. His legal name had turned out to be Kenneth Paul Stanley, he was eight years older than he'd told Amy he was, and officers were currently investigating his suspected involvement in various other jurisdictions for multiple other cold case crimes and murders.

As they pulled up in front of Pine Crest, Amy could see Walter sitting on a bench in front of the home, arms crossed and hands covered in large woolen mittens. Jackson pulled the car to a stop. But as he and Amy got out, Walter stood and waved both of them off.

"Stay there," he called. He ambled toward them. Despite the fact he was trying his best to frown, Amy could see the unmistakable twinkle of joy in the old man's eyes. "No need to get yourself out. I'll come to you."

"Yes, sir," Jackson said with a smile. He went around to the back door, opened it and pulled out a wooden box from under the driver's seat.

Amy gave Walter a warm hug.

"How are you doing?" Walter asked. "Jackson taking care of you all?"

"He is," Amy said.

Jackson stood back and waited as Walter stuck

his head in the open backseat and said hello to Skye and Hudson in turn. Then the older man turned to Jackson.

"So, what's all this about?" he asked. "You called and said you had something for me?"

"Yes, sir." Jackson handed him the wooden box. "Police released Gordon Donnelly's possessions from the evidence locker today, and when they contacted his granddaughter, she said the family wanted you to have these."

Walter took off his mittens and opened the box. His eyes misted as he looked down at the collection of Second World War medals nestled in the blue velvet inside. He wiped his hand over the back of his eyes, opened his mouth, then closed it again and patted Jackson on the back.

"Thank you," Walter said.

"You're welcome," Jackson replied. "Thank you for being so relentless in making sure this case wasn't forgotten."

Walter nodded. Then he glanced at Amy.

"This man is a good man, you know," Walter told her and pointed at Amy.

Amy's eyes searched the strong and tender lines of Jackson's face. "I know."

Jackson and Amy drove in comfortable silence back to the cottage. Jackson laid his hand in the space between them. She took it and their fingers linked so naturally it was as if their hands had been made to hold each other. She'd lost track of how many times she and Jackson had held hands, hugged or gently kissed goodbye over the past few months. All she knew is that there was something safe and comforting about having him near. She'd never felt this before.

When they reached the cottage, there was an unfamiliar truck parked in the driveway. She carried Skye to the house, and Jackson held open the door for her. She quickly realized who the pickup belonged to as Nippy made a beeline toward them. The two dogs greeted each other in a flurry of enthusiastically wagging tails. Thankfully, Gemma had made peace with having the K-9s around, although Amy knew that in Gemma's heart, no dog could ever hold a candle to her Reepi. Amy could hear the parrot chirping cheerfully from his perch in the living room. He'd been traveling with Gemma to and from the store since the break-in, and was no longer there alone overnight. They found Finnick and Gemma sitting at the dining table. When Jackson had told her that something important had come up for Gemma, she hadn't imagined it involved Jackson's boss. Gemma and Finnick stood.

"How did everything go with the doctor and with Walter?" Gemma asked.

"Wonderfully." Amy gave her a one-armed

hug and slipped Skye into Gemma's outstretched hands. Then she turned to Finnick.

"It's nice to see you again, Inspector," Amy said. "To what do we owe the pleasure?"

"I'm here to offer Gemma a job," Finnick said.

And the huge smile and slightly overwhelmed look on Gemma's face told Amy that she'd said yes.

"I've finally got permission to launch a dedicated Cold Case Task Force," Finnick went on. "I'm planning to pull in officers from across the province and around the country to tackle many of the cases that have gone unsolved for far too long. I'm hoping to not only bring justice to a lot of families who've been waiting for it, but also to help restore confidence in our commitment that no victim of crime will be forgotten."

Amy turned to Gemma. "You're going to become a cop?"

"No way," Gemma said, with a laugh. "I'm very happy to be a private investigator. I'm going to join the task force as a civilian consultant and family liaison."

"As Gemma rightly pointed out, there are a lot of people who have lost confidence in police," Finnick said. "So, Gemma's going to be an integral part of building trust, and I'm going to be partnering her with law enforcement officers on some cases. I've already got plans to talk to Blake and Caleb about the team, as well as to try roping in Jackson here. But I wanted to talk with Gemma first."

Joy filled Amy's heart as she looked from one shining face to the next. "That's incredible."

"Yeah, and an answer to a whole lot of prayers," Gemma said. "But this does mean I'm going to need your help more than ever to keep the store running."

"You can count on me," Amy said. Already the small turquoise barn full of books and artwork was beginning to feel like home. Amy had been helping at the bookstore on and off over the past few months as she was able, and had designated a special space on the wall in the main room to be a roving display for local artists—including some incredibly talented children, teenagers, senior citizens, painters, sketch artists and photographers to display and sell their art. "We'll work it all out, and it'll be amazing."

Thanksgiving filled her heart for the immeasurable prayers that had been answered in the past few months, and yet an odd aching in her heart told her that there was one thing still missing.

"Do you mind watching Skye for a moment?" she asked Gemma. "I need to talk to your brother about something."

"Absolutely," Gemma said. "No problem."

Jackson leaned toward Amy. "Everything okay?" he asked softly.

"Not quite yet," she said. "But it will be."

Together they walked out the sliding glass door onto the back porch, down the steps and out toward the water until they reached the end of the dock. There they stood, side by side. A crisp autumn breeze cut through her jacket. She leaned her shoulder against Jackson and he put his arm around her.

"So, are you going to join the cold case team?" Amy asked.

Jackson grinned. "Probably, if it doesn't get in the way of me being around here to help give you guys backup when you need it."

Lord, I was so worried of wasting my own life that I just recklessly threw myself into every adventure I could find. I never even stopped to look and see if there was a path that You'd laid out for me or think about what I wanted for my life. But since my life was forced to slow down, I've finally been able to see what I want and where I want to be.

She glanced at the incredible man beside her.

"I'm ready," she said.

Jackson turned. Confusion crossed his face, then amazement and finally hope.

"Are you saying what I think you're saying?" he asked.

She turned to face him.

"I'm ready to start the next chapter of my life," she said, "and I don't want to waste a single moment of it." She took both of his hands in hers and looked up at the strong, handsome man she knew, without a shadow of a doubt, that she wanted to see for the rest of her life. "I wake up every morning thinking of your face and I fall asleep every night grateful that you are in my life. For once, I'm not leaping blindly. I love you, Jackson. I've known it deep in my heart every day for months. And I want to spend the rest of my life with you."

"I love you too," Jackson said. "I always have and I always will."

Slowly, he pulled his hands from hers. Then he reached into his jacket pocket, pulled out a small box and opened it. There, lay a simple gold and diamond engagement ring.

She laughed. "How long have you been carrying that around?"

"Months," Jackson said. "Ever since the moment I knew that, more than anything else in the world, I wanted to marry you, Amy Scout. I love you."

"I love you too."

"And you'll be my wife?"

"Absolutely."

He slid the ring onto her finger. She wound

her hands around his neck. He wrapped his arms around her and held her close.

"Are you sure about this?" Jackson asked.

"As confident as I am in the ground beneath our feet, the sky above us and the air we breathe."

"Me too," Jackson said.

He kissed her deeply. She kissed him back and knew with every part of her that she was where she was meant to be.

* * * * *

If you enjoyed Cold Case Tracker
*Be sure to discover more titles
by Maggie K. Black*

Available at LoveInspired.com*!*

Dear Reader,

I've mentioned my grandfather many times in these pages. He was my hero, my favorite story-teller and a part of every book I write. The "K" in my name is a tribute to him. It's been almost twenty years since he passed away and I think of him every day.

My grandfather lived to be 81, which at the time I thought was a wonderfully long life to live. Then, a few weeks ago, his older brother passed away at the age of 103.

The family had three daughters and seven sons. My grandfather and four of his brothers made the local paper during the Second World War for all serving in the Canadian Armed Forces together. My childhood is filled to the brim with happy memories of my great-uncles and great-aunts, their children and grandchildren. Now, there's only one son remaining, whose granddaughter is also an aspiring romance writer. But even though some of my grandfather's siblings passed long before I was born, their names, faces and stories were also a huge part of my childhood.

Their lives are a reminder to me that we don't always know the course our lives will take or the impact they'll have.

I pray that God will help us all live our lives to the fullest and to be a blessing to all those our lives touch.

Thanks again for sharing this journey with me.
Maggie